LEAD HUNGRY LOBOS

LEAD HUNGRY LOBOS

BURT ARTHUR

ISBN-13: 978-1-954840-67-6

Published by
Cutting Edge Books
PO Box 8212
Calabasas, CA 91372
www.cuttingedgebooks.com

TABLE OF CONTENTS

CHAPTER ONE

THE TOWN WITHOUT A NAME

THE TOWN lay sprawled out in the bright morning sun on a flat land with nothing between it and the distant horizon but a vast expanse of earth that was the open range. It was a tiny town, hardly more than a settlement, with some two score drab shacks and lean-to's comprising the town whose entire life and activity appeared to be concentrated along the stunted length of what was evidently a street. Actually it bore little resemblance to a street; there were no sidewalks and no gutter.

Marshall, cantering into town, halted his mount when they came abreast of what appeared to be a sign-post. A close-up examination revealed that there was no name on the warped piece of board. There were, however, some faint tracings or outlines of letters which had long since faded out. Marshall's eyes ranged over the street. The echo of his horse's hoofs hung in the still air for another brief moment and faded away presently; then there was no further sound save the creaking of his saddle and the impatient pawing of his mount's hoof on the ground. A tin smokestack that reared its blunt, blackened snoot above the slanting roof of a shack at the far end of the street caught his eye. Suddenly smoke belched from the stack and curled lazily upward into the sky.

"That's somthin'," Marshall muttered. "Reckon it ain't deserted after all."

He nudged his horse with his knees and the big black jogged away. They came abreast of the only substantial-looking structure on the street, a two-story high building with a sign that read "Hotel" hanging over its doorway, and the word "Saloon" painted in white letters on its street-floor windows. Marshall jerked the black to a stop. There was a man in the doorway of the saloon, a man with a drooping mustache who looked up from his perch atop an upended beer keg and who raised his right hand in a tired and unenthusiastic greeting. Marshall swung the black over to the hitching rail in front of the saloon, and eased himself in the saddle.

"Howdy," he said.

The man answered with a nod of head.

"What's th' name o' this town?"

"Ain't got 'ny," came the reply. "As a matter o' fact, Stranger, it ain't never had 'ny."

Marshall shoved his hat up from his eyes.

"You don't say!"

The man nodded again, gravely.

"Feller named Rafferty settled here some time back. He worked f'r th' stagecoach comp'ny. Seems he was a driver fer 'em till some Indians jumped 'im an' messed 'im up a bit with their tomahawks. Th' comp'ny give 'im a job settin' up a way station fer 'em here—y'know, supplyin' 'em with relief horses. He put up a shack an' somethin' uv a corral, but that was about all. Anyway, he never give th' place a name an' neither did 'nybody else. An' that th' way it's been. S-ay, partner, what would it set me back t' buy a horse somethin' like th' one you're straddlin'?"

"Dunno. I ain't never tried 't buy another one."

"Wa-al, wanna sell yourn?"

"Nope."

"I'll go as high as fifty bucks fer her."

"Fer him."

"Huh? Oh, yeah, sure—fer him. How 'bout it? You int'rested?"

"Nope."

The man grinned.

"You'd be a danged fool if you sold him. Dunno where you'd buy 'nother one 'round here. Fact is there ain't a critter worthy o' bein' called a horse 'round these parts. I oughta know. I've been lookin' fer a good horse fer a long time, an' outside o' yourn I ain't seen anythin' worth stablin'. You better keep both o' your eyes on him while you're here. If you don't, he's li'ble t' disappear all uva sudden."

"I'll take my chances on it that he won't do anything o' th' kind. He don't like strangers an' he's li'ble t' kick th' head offa anybody who tries t' touch 'im,"

"Oh, yeah?" The man laughed lightly. "Glad you mentioned that. I aim t' go on livin' fer a while yet, an' I'd sure hate t' hafta go on through life without a head."

"Reckon he won't do 'ny disappearin' then, eh?"

"Nope."

"Good. S-ay, there any other towns around?"

"Which way you goin'?"

"West."

"On'y Rainbow, an' that's about eighty miles fr'm here."

"Uh-huh, an' what's this Rainbow place like?"

The man eyed him for a moment; he looked sharply at the brace of heavy black Colts that hung low against Marshall's thighs.

"You hightailin' it?"

"Nope. I'm peaceable. Actu'lly I'm headed fer California an' I allus like t' know what's ahead o' me."

"Wa-al, Rainbow an' this hell-hole are kinda alike, 'cept that Rainbow's a heap bigger. B'sides, there's good, rich ranch land 'round Rainbow an' that gives th' citizens a chance t' makes some dough t' spend. This place is deader'n all hell an' just as busted."

"You said Rainbow an' this—this place—were kinda alike?"

The man climbed to his feet. He sauntered outside, glanced at the sky mechanically, leaned against the rail.

"Both o' th'm are sore spots an' oughta be wiped off th' map. That's how they're alike, see?"

Marshall "saw," and indicated it by nodding understandingly.

"Look up that street," the man continued. Marshall followed the man's eyes. "Lookit it. Th' hull danged place is just fallin' apart. An' why? 'Cause there ain't anything in this place but drunks an' passin' through badmen hightailin' either west or east."

"Uh-huh. Still, there must be some decent folks among them?"

The man shrugged his shoulders.

"Y'mean there must be some that ain't as bad as th' others. Yeah, I suppose there are some, but they ain't too many fer a feller t' count on one hand without runnin' over t' th' other hand."

"Some paint an' some plankin' where th' old wood's rotted away might do this place some good," Marshall remarked. "Anybody ever try 'em?"

"Yeah, sure, one feller did. But he didn't get 'ny good outta all 'is work."

"How come?"

"Wa-al, it allus seemed kinda funny t' me, but right when he got his place t' lookin' like somethin', doggoned if it didn't catch fire an' burn down. Danged near burned down th' rest o' th' place, too. Everyb'dy said it was 'n accident. I had diff'rent ideas about it but I wasn't goin' outta my way fer 'n argument, so I just went along th' way th' others said an' kept th' peace. You passin' through or you plannin' t' stay over fer a while?"

"That depends. Got a decent place fer a feller t' bed down?"

"Oh, sure!"

"Good. I haven't been in a bed fer a week. Right now I could sleep fer a week t' make up fer lost time."

"Give you your pick o' any o' th' rooms at five bucks a throw."

"How about some grub?"

"I c'n fix you up on that, too."

"Swell!"

"S'ppose you climb down, Stranger, an' lead your horse 'round th' back t' th' stable? Then you come on in inside an' I'll get t' work hustlin' up somethin' fer you t' eat."

Marshall swung himself out of the saddle.

"Oh, yeah—what's your name, Mister?"

"Marshall."

"Uh-huh. Gotta write it down. That's th'law, y'know, fer hotels. I don't see 'ny sense to it, since there ain't 'ny lawmen 'round these parts, but I'm willin' t' do like I'm told. Saves a feller from trouble."

"That's right."

"My name's Jones," the man went on. "Si Jones. Th' old man named me Sylvester after some judge or somethin', but I ain't been called that since I was able t' stand up an' fight back. Sylvester! Ain't that one Godawful name? I made Si out uv it an' I've lived my life as Si an' I'm doggoned if I don't die Si! Go 'head, Marshall; you're tired an' hungry an' I'm jawin' away like 'n old woman leanin' over a back fence 'stead o' fixin' you up. That's right; foller that alley straight down till you come t' th' stable."

Marshall awoke with a start. He rolled over reluctantly, lay on his back for a brief moment longer and listened. He heard loud voices again—this time he thought they sounded just a bit louder than before—and he propped himself up on his elbows. There was a loud crash and he swung his legs over the side of the bed and stood up, stubbed his toes on his boots and cursed under his breath and sat down hastily, rubbing the bruised foot tenderly. Presently he reached for the boots and drew them on; then he stood up again. He remembered there was a window close to the bed, groped for it in the darkness and finally found it. He clutched the lowered shade and yanked it. It shot out of his hand with surprising suddenness and swept upward and rolled itself up with a whirring sound. He threw open the window and looked down into the street.

It was dark and deserted beneath a starless sky and a cloud-obscured moon. The shacks along the street were darkened, too, and in the distorting night-light they loomed up curiously odd-shaped. From the windows of the saloon directly below him rays of yellowish lamplight streaked out to form an uneven rim of eerie light. He heard a shot, a cry. There was a moment's hushed silence; then as he watched, two men came running out of the saloon. He saw them whirl around the building to the alley. They reappeared shortly, mounted, wheeled their horses, lashed them and sent them racing up the street and into the blanketing darkness.

Marshall started toward the door, stopped and retraced his steps to the bed, groped for the bed-post, caught up his gun belt from around the post, whipped it around his waist and buckled it on, and turned again toward the door. In the darkness he stumbled over a chair and fell over it. He cursed aloud and got up, sending the offending chair spinning across the room. It collided with the far wall, caromed off and toppled over to the floor. He reached the door and fumbled gropingly for the bolt lock, found it finally and drew it back, then opened the door and burst into the hallway. Fortunately there was a light in the hallway; a swinging overhead lamp furnished a dim light. He ran down the hallway to the stairway, stopped briefly and peered over the banister.

His eyes widened. On the floor directly below the stair well lay a huddled figure, a man with one arm outflung. He knew at once that it was Jones. He raced down the stairs to the saloon keeper's side, bent over him briefly, turned him over on his back. There was an ugly bruise on Jones' forehead—doubtless the result of a blow with the butt of a gun—and a ragged smear of blood on his shirt-front. Marshall opened the man's shirt and unbuttoned his undershirt; there was a bullet hole through Jones' heart.

Marshall came erect again. A piece of torn green string on the floor just beyond Jones' limp body caught his eye. He picked it up rather mechanically, toyed with it for a moment, then eyed it suddenly, sharply, remembering in that moment where he had seen it before, or perhaps another piece just like it. He recalled that when he had paid Jones for his breakfast, the saloon keeper had produced a canvas bag from his hip pocket, untied the green string around it and dropped Marshall's silver dollar into the bag. It was clear now that the motive for Jones' killing was robbery; it was clear too that his killers had taken the canvas bag, and that he would have to locate the bag in order to identify the murderers.

Marshall shoved the string into his pocket. He turned on his heel, strode to the doorway, halted there briefly and looked back at the dead man, then went out. Minutes later there was a clatter of hoofs toward the rear of the saloon. Presently the rested black, prancing and eager to run, came up the alley with Marshall astride him. They loped into the street, wheeled and darted away into the night.

Dawn on the range!

Drab, empty, leaden skies overhead with no light in the limitless expanse to herald the approach of day. A brisk, chilling wind whipped southward over the range, droned through the wild, coarse grass; and curled-up, sun-browned vagrant leaves and tiny bits of broken twigs and brush, caught up by the wind and whisked through space, dropped limply to the ground when the swift wind swerved and changed the course and direction of its flight. Top soil and dust spun by in the wake of the wind, and the black, halted atop a rise that commanded a broad view of the range, whinnied, and failing to obtain an understanding and sympathetic response from his rider, pawed the ground impatiently.

As Marshall's eyes probed the distant reaches of the range, a faint light gleamed in the sky like a flickering candle flaming briefly in the wind. There was no immediate change, either in the sky or on the earth; it was minutes later when the light flashed again, this time stronger and steadier as though defying the wind. Then there was a sudden brightening. Night shadows were whisked away. The very earth, the rocks, the grass became substantial things, each in its own right; now too the sky itself glowed and a rosy hue filled the horizon. There was even a faint stirring up above, and the earth caught a fleeting glimpse of the sun and the dawn became day. The chilling wind died down, disappeared, and a heartening warmth settled over the earth. Marshall stiffened when he saw two horsemen suddenly ride into view about half a mile to the south.

There was a certain furtiveness about the two men; they seemed uneasy and they twisted around in their saddles continuously as if they expected pursuers to appear over the horizon at any given moment. Their uneasiness communicated itself to Marshall and he watched them through narrowed eyes. He had finally caught up with his quarries. In the night light they had managed to elude him; now, in the bright morning sun, there would be no further escape. They might postpone the accounting they would have to make, but in the end payment of the most exacting nature would be made.

"Awright!" he said suddenly, but the black showed no surprise. He had already sensed that his rider had finally overtaken the men they had sought through the long dark hours of the night. His head came up and he waited for Marshall's word to swing into action.

"Go 'head!" Marshall said, and the alert black bounded away. He was eager to run, and now that the opportunity for unrestrained speed was thrust into his very jaws, he flashed over the ground at a whirlwind pace. He snorted loudly like a runaway train flashing over a cleared right-of-way, its whistle trumpeting its flight. But now the swift clatter of hoofs had reached the two horsemen. They turned as one and stared hard. Again as one they lashed their mounts, spurred them on desperately, for the chase was on. But there was no denying the thundering black. He swept southward in a furious rhythmic drum-roll of lightning hoof beats that swelled as he lessened the distance between pursuer and pursued. Five hundred yards, four hundred, and then the intervening gap had been narrowed to some three hundred yards.

One of the fugitives twisted around in the saddle. His gun gleamed in his raised hand. He snapped a shot and the bullet furrowed the ground fifteen feet from the pounding black. A second bullet skidded over the ground, caromed off the side of a half-buried rock and zoomed away in deflected flight. A third shot, and that far wilder than the others, followed... Still there was no answering fire from Marshall. His failure to shoot back was maddening to his quarries. In his cold and unresponsive plan they sensed his complete confidence in the black's ability to overtake them and ride them into the ground. In desperation the man who had fired at him bent low over his mount, urged him on; when the horse stumbled and paused only momentarily, the thoroughly frightened fugitive lashed him cruelly. The pain-maddened horse leaped forward with a sudden burst of speed, leaving the second man far behind. Now Marshall was less than two hundred yards behind him. A Colt flashed in the bright sunlight. It thundered deadeningly and the lagging man's horse stumbled and fell, pitching his rider over his head.

The man struck the ground heavily, crashed on his left shoulder and toppled over. Somehow he managed to scramble to his feet. His companion pulled up in a dust-raising stop. The dismounted man, running like a frightened deer, came abreast of him, caught the hand thrust out to him and vaulted up behind his mate.

But now Marshall's plan of retaliation came to light. Cold, deliberate, and completely unhurried, he raised his gun a second time. The Colt roared mightily and the overburdened horse ahead of him screamed and plunged to his knees, hurling both men over his head. There was a frenzied scrambling to feet and both men started to run. The black came up behind them; however, with Marshall, holding him in check, they maintained a distance of some twenty yards behind the fugitives.

The Colt flamed and a bullet kicked up the dirt just ahead of one man, who jumped wildly. His companion whirled and threw a canvas bag. It struck the ground and silver coins spewed out of it. The first man panted to a stop, his chest heaving; he turned and thrust his arms skyward in token of surrender. The second man skidded to a halt and turned around with his hands over his head. The black halted.

"Awright," Marshall said coldly. "Reckon this is th' end o' th' trail fer you two polecats. Keep your hands high an' don't try 'ny tricks 'less you want me t' blast yuh apart."

He nudged the black with his knees and the big horse went forward again, slowly and warily. The muzzle of the Colt in Marshall's right hand gaped at the two men. They eyed it fearfully, and it seemed to widen as they stared at it.

"Which one o' you skunks killed Jones?" Marshall demanded.

There was no reply, merely a shifting of weight from one leg to the other.

"Don't suppose it'll make much diff'rence," Marshall continued coldly. "Both o' you'll swing fer it."

One of the fugitives raised his head; he was surprisingly young and white-faced. There was terror in his eyes.

"No!" he gasped.

He backed away, turned suddenly and fled. Marshall made no move; even the alert black, ready to resume the pursuit, seemed surprised. He waited expectantly for Marshall's signal. Marshall was eyeing the second man, goading him with silence, taunting him to do something. The seconds passed, and finally the man wheeled and ran. Marshall nudged the black and the big horse bounded off, only to have Marshall pull him back and hold him down to a mere trot. The younger man, running first one way, then that, in his frantic efforts to escape, suddenly swung northward. His companion jerked out his gun, yelled something and fired twice. When both shots went wild, he drew back his arm and hurled his gun at the black, but it fell far short. He dashed on, fell into a jogging lope.

It was a strange affair. There was Marshall astride the black, and the big horse was completely bewildered. He couldn't seem to understand the situation. Then there were the two fugitives, one of them a hundred yards away and bearing more and more toward the north, while his companion, trotting dog-like, turned northward, too, unconsciously perhaps. The sun rose higher; perhaps from its lofty perch it too had been watching the "chase" and now, puzzled, had decided to follow along in order to see the outcome.

The younger man stumbled down an incline. He did not reappear. It was some minutes later when a muffled shot rang out. The panting fugitive just ahead of Marshall jerked to an open-mouthed stop.

"Reckon he won't hang," Marshall said curtly. "Which one o' you did th' actu'l killing?"

"Him," the winded man breathed.

Marshall's eyes glinted.

"Mebbe," he snapped. "But you had Jones' moneybag. Th' chances are you put 'im up t' doin' th' shootin'; then you took the money. Wa-al, long's you hang, everything'll be squared up, leastways as much as we c'n without bringin' Jones back t' life."

The man stumbled on again. They went down the incline. At the bottom of it, as Marshall expected, they found the first man. He lay out-sprawled, dead, with his lifeless hand still clutching his gun. Marshall halted the black.

"Awright," he said briskly. "He's dead. His debt's paid. We'll go back an' see that you square up, too."

The man stared at him. He was worn out. He stumbled up to his dead companion, looked down at him, then raised his head and looked first at Marshall, then at the Colt in Marshall's hand. For a minute he was motionless, rooted to the ground; then he bent down, and took the gun from the hand of the dead man. Marshall wheeled the black and rode slowly up the incline.

"Awright," he said. "Reckon we c'n go on t' Rainbow now."

There was a shot at the bottom of the incline. The black stopped and Marshall twisted around in the saddle and looked down. The second of the fugitives lay in a limp heap. Marshall watched him for a minute, warily. He saw the man's right leg twitch briefly; then he lay still. Marshall settled himself in the saddle. The black went on again. They reached level ground again and turned westward. Marshall glanced skyward. The sun had moved on again, evidence that its curiosity had been satisfied.

CHAPTER TWO

THE COMING OF MARSHALL

THE TRAIL wound steadily upward through the thick, lush grass and the multi-hued flowers that dotted the steep hillside in a riotous profusion of color. At the top of the hill were white, fleecy clouds, giving one the impression that the sky was resting on the hill.

The big black horse snorted protestingly. He had done more hill climbing this day than on any other day that he could recall, and now he was tired and winded and almost convinced that it would never end. Astride him, Marshall shifted himself a bit in the saddle.

"I know, I know," he said wearily. "You're plumb wore out an' so am I, but this can't last ferever, y'know. We're bound t' reach level ground sooner or later, so you might's well shut up an' save your breath an' just keep goin' till we do."

The black voiced an answering and evidently dissatisfied snort, but Marshall disregarded it. He looked up suddenly. The air was surprisingly cooler now, proof that they were nearing the top of the hill. The big horse noticed it and raised his head, too; he even quickened his pace. Then suddenly they were on level ground again.

"There y'are," Marshall said. "Just like I told you."

He sat upright again in the saddle; the black's tiredness seemed to disappear and he loped away effortlessly. They swept over the grassy level for some ten, fifteen minutes, and had covered about a mile when Marshall pulled the black to a halt. They had come to the end of the level ground. Below them, spreading away at the base of a gentle slope, was a sprawling town. Marshall pushed his dust-smudged hat back from his eyes.

"Wa-al, what d'you know!" he muttered in surprised tones. "I woulda been willin' t' bet there wasn't anything b'tween these hills but more hills. 'Stead, there's a town lazyin' down there just waitin' fer us t' drop in an' say howdy!"

He settled himself deeply in the saddle.

"Go 'head!" he said.

The black went on again, down the grassy incline; then they were trotting onto hard, barren ground that presently became a street. The big horse whinnied but there was no answering hail; his hoofs echoed metallically on the ground. There were stores on both sides of the street. Above one doorway hung a sign whose faded letters formed the word "EAT"; twenty feet beyond it was a double-windowed store with the single legend: "BANK," daubed on its dirty panes. Halfway down the street was a two-story structure, the tallest building in the town. There was a sagging porch in front of it, and a huge side that read "HOTEL" hung between the two middle windows on the upper floor. There were hitching posts and rails at various points along the curb, but they were completely unused. Marshall halted the black. He was puzzled and the expression on his bronzed face reflected it.

"Funny," he muttered. He twisted around for a moment; then he settled himself again in the saddle. "Doggone funny, if anybody should ask me. Not a sign o' life anywheres. Looks like one o' them ghost towns I've heard tell about."

He stiffened instinctively when he heard a door creak open somewhere behind him along the street, and turned around. From the doorway of the bank a man with a half raised rifle in his hands peered out at him for a moment, then he withdrew his head. The door slammed shut and the jarring noise echoed the length of the street. Marshall frowned.

"Nice feller," he mumbled. "Looks me over from top t' bottom; then he pulls in 'is head without sayin' a word o' greeting."

He wheeled the black and rode slowly down the street, pulled up in front of the bank and dismounted stiffly. He hitched up his pants and trudged across the wooden sidewalk. The black turned his head and followed Marshall with his eyes. The wooden planking that formed the sidewalk was warped and it creaked dismally beneath Marshall's step. He glanced at the word "BANK" on the window pane, halted when he reached the closed door. He jerked it impatiently; when it refused to open he frowned again and rapped on it sharply.

"Hey!" he yelled. "Open up! Y'got comp'ny!"

There was no response. He gave the door knob a vicious twist.

"Hey!" he yelled a second time.

The door was suddenly opened. In the doorway stood the man with the rifle, and this time the weapon was levelled. Its muzzle gaped menacingly at Marshall's chest. The man behind the rifle was grey-haired and nervously quick-eyed.

"Howdy," Marshall said curtly. The man did not answer. His finger seemed to tighten around the trigger of the rifle. "What kind uva place is this, huh? This th' way you us'ally greet strangers 'round these parts?"

"Who—who are you?"

"Oh, so you have got a tongue, eh? My name's Marshall."

"What d'you want?"

"Somethin' t' eat an' drink an' a place t' sleep."

The rifle was lowered the barest bit.

"You'd better keep goin', Mister," the man said. "This ain't th' safest place fer anybody t' be at."

There was a light step behind him. Marshall's eyes swept past the man. A girl came forward. She, too, carried a rifle.

"What is it, Tom?" she asked. She avoided Marshall's eyes, looked him over appraisingly, halted her eyes lingeringly on the brace of heavy black Colts that hung low against his lean thighs. "Who is this man?"

"Says his name's Marshall an' that he's lookin' f'r some grub an' a place t' bed down."

Marshall grinned lightly.

"That goes fer my horse, too," he said.

The girl's eyes came up to meet his. Hers were soft and brown but troubled. For a second time she looked down at his holstered guns.

"One o' you mind tellin' me what's goin' on around here?" he asked. "What's all th' mystery about?"

"You can put down your rifle, Tom," the girl said.

The grey-haired man backed deeper into the store. The girl came forward to the doorway. For a moment she and Marshall eyed each other; then presently his eyes ranged past her. Behind her he could see overturned chairs, a smashed table and papers scattered on the floor. He looked surprised but he made no comment.

"We didn't mean to be rude," he heard her say, and he looked at her again.

"That's awright," he replied. "Sorry I busted in on you like this, but th' old feller was th' on'y human I saw."

"Yes," she said patiently. "We're the only ones left in Rainbow. Everyone else has gone. I think it would be wise for you to go, too."

"That so? Why?"

"Things are liable to happen around here," she said significantly.

"From th' looks o' this place," he answered wryly, "I'd say they have happened a'ready."

"We expect them to be even worse."

"You don't say!"

"That's why you'd better go," she concluded.

He hooked his thumbs in his gun belt.

"What's s'posed t' follow th' tornado or whatever it was that hit here?" he asked.

"Fire," she said simply.

His eyebrows arched.

"Oh, yeah?"

She nodded mutely, wearily.

"Look," he said. "S'pose you tell me what this bus'ness is all about? Mebbe I c'n do somethin'."

She smiled wanly and shook her head.

"I'm afraid there isn't anything anyone can do now."

"I'm still willin' t' try."

She shrugged slender shoulders.

"I don't suppose there can be any harm in telling you. As you probably noticed, this is a bank. My father owned it. Anyway, we were robbed the other night. The depositors—they're cattlemen—we-ll, curiously enough, the very next morning every one of them appeared and clamored for their money."

"Nice spot fer your Dad t' be in with all th' dough gone," he said.

Her face clouded.

"Dad tried to explain to them what had happened. He promised to make good the money somehow; however, he begged them to give him some time to raise it. They wouldn't listen," she said bitterly. "They accused him of robbing the bank. Oh, they said some perfectly terrible things to Dad."

He nodded grimly.

"They were cattlemen awright," he said understandingly. "They're allus too thick-headed t' listen t' reason. They ain't got 'ny more sense than their steers."

"Dad finally lost his temper," the girl continued. "He ordered them out. There was a fight. Dad was shot."

"That was a tough break. Was he hit bad?"

"He's dead," she said simply.

His lips thinned.

"Killin' him off just about killed off their chances o' ever gettin' their money back. but knowin' cattlemen an' how they op'rate, I wouldn't expect them t' figger that out, leastways not right off."

"They didn't look at Dad's death that way. They sent me word that they'd come for their money today."

"They did, eh? An' where are you supposed t' get it from?" he demanded.

"I don't think they gave that any thought."

"That all th' message they sent you?"

"Yes, practically all. Of course, they added a threat to it."

" 'Course. I'd expect th'm t' do that. What was th' threat?" he asked.

"If I can't produce the money when they come for it today, they're going to burn Rainbow to the ground."

"Just like that, eh? Is that why everybody hightailed it?"

"Yes," she replied. "But I can't say that I blame them. The Wades are bad, thoroughly and cruelly bad, so it isn't surprising that everyone's afraid of them."

"Everybody 'cept you an' th' old feller. Who are these Wades?" he asked.

"Oh, they own the Bar-O Ranch. It's the biggest spread in the county. The Wade boys, Ed and Jim, are twins, and they're equally bad."

"What about th' law? Don't it hamper their style none?"

"Not in the slightest. The Wades do things around here to suit themselves."

"Yeah, but what about th' sheriff? He do 'nything 'bout clippin' their wings?"

The girl's lip curled scornfully.

"Sheriff Hodges is their cousin. Actually, he owes his job to them," she explained.

"So that's how it is in Rainbow!"

"Yes."

"Where's this Hodges feller now? Don't tell me he's high-tailed it, too?"

"He has! Whenever anything happens, the sheriff is out of town. We've become quite accustomed to that situation. Of course, when things quiet down, he always returns."

"Y'got some set-up in this town, awright! Say, who's th' old feller?"

"Tom? Oh, he's just an old friend. He was a storekeeper here in town, but the Wades ruined him. Dad took him in and he's been with us ever since. I don't know what I'd have done without him."

"Uh-huh. Oh, yeah—what's your name?"

"It's Grant, Frances Grant. However, everyone calls me Fran," she answered. "But you'd better be going now. I shouldn't have kept you here this long."

He wheeled abruptly and marched to the waiting black at the curb. The big horse turned his head and watched him jerk his rifle out of the leather sheath that hung on his saddle below the dangling right stirrup.

"Got a place fer him?" Marshall asked over his shoulder, nodding toward the idling horse.

Fran's eyes widened.

"You mean you're—"

"I sure am stayin' put in Rainbow," he said with a grin. "I've allus wanted t' work in a bank. Here's just th' chance I've been waitin' fer, an' I'm doggoned if I don't grab it while th' grabbin's good."

"But—"

"No buts about it," he said. He came striding back to the doorway. "You've hired y'self a new teller. Mind if I step inside? Might be a good idea t' kinda get organized t' receive th' customers, y'know!"

It was late afternoon, a cool, oppressively silent and tensed interlude between day and night. The lengthening shadows had already appeared and draped themselves over the hastily closed-down town. A tiny piece of paper, caught up by a swirling gust of wind, sped wildly and blindly along the gutter; when the wind died down, the paper dropped limply, twisted and exhausted, against the curb. Inside the bank, the chairs and the smashed table had been removed. Marshall, his thumbs hooked in his gun belt, lounged idly and impatiently in the open doorway. He looked up quickly when he heard a noise; it was the drab "EAT" sign flapping in the breeze on its rusty hinges.

He heard a light step overhead on the roof—Fran's. He had insisted that she and old Tom remove themselves from the premises, for he was certain that there would be some kind of outbreak—gun-play he expected, even though he hadn't said so—when the Wades arrived. Fran of course had refused. He in turn had insisted even more firmly than before; and she finally agreed when he suggested that she and Tom move up to the roof. With them up there, he had pointed out, he would be better able to cope with the situation, especially if the Wades attacked in numbers. From their posts on the roof they could add a helpful rifle fire in the event of a frontal attack. He stiffened when he heard a distant rumble of horses' hoofs.

"Uh-huh," he said aloud. "Reckon th' Wades are fin'lly comin'."

He stepped back, closed the door, vaulted the low counter and straightened up behind it. The clatter of hoofs swelled. He heard a thumping on the roof, a prearranged signal to warn him of the Wades' approach. Then iron-shod hoofs filled the street with a metallic thunder. A group of hard-riding horsemen swept past the bank at a full gallop. Dust swirled around them, then over their heads. A moment later two of them came riding back. Marshall saw them pull up at the curb, saw them dismount.

"One o' th'm's bigger'n a bear," he muttered as he watched them saunter toward the door. "Reckon he's one o' th' Wades. Th' other feller's a heap smaller but even more ornery-lookin' than th' big one."

He leaned back against the wall. The door was flung open and the two men pushed their way in. Marshall straightened up, grinned and waved his hand.

"Howdy, gents," he called, "Glad t' see you. Mind closin' th' door, partner?"

The big man gave him a hard look, and he and his companion exchanged glances. When the former nodded, the second man kicked the door shut.

"Thanks, partner," Marshall said amiably. "Now, then, gents, what c'n I do for you? Talk right up. Don't cost a danged cent t' ask questions, y'know."

The big man frowned, shifted his holster, then he came lumbering up to the counter.

"Where's Fran Grant?" he demanded.

Marshall grinned again.

"Gone, my friend," he answered. "But don't ask me where. Feller ain't supposed t' ask a lady where she's goin', y'know. He's liable t' get told."

He laughed loudly, and Wade scowled. Marshall shook his head sadly.

"Sure beats all hell how some fellers c'n tell a joke an' have everyb'dy listenin', rollin' on th' floor," he said sheepishly. "When I tell 'em—heck, they fall flatter'n a pancake. Wonder if it's th' jokes or just me?"

Wade's lip curled.

"I wonder," he said coldly. He leaned against the counter. "Who'n hell are you?"

Marshall's eyebrows arched in surprise.

"Me?"

"Who d'you think I mean?"

"Couldn't be anybody else but me, could it—bein' that I'm th' on'y one b'hind here?"

"Waal?"

"Huh? Oh, I'm Marshall. What's your handle, partner?"

"Wade!" the big man snapped. "What are you doin' here?"

Marshall's chest swelled.

"Heck, Mister, I'm president, gen'ral manager, even th' porter," he announced, and tapped himself on the chest. "Fact o' th' matter is, partner, I'm what you might call th' hull danged works. Somethin' I c'n do fer you? Wanna make a deposit or somethin'?"

Wade's companion came forward now and tugged at the big man's sleeve. Wade and he moved back from the counter and conferred in whispers for a moment; then Wade nodded. The other man turned and trudged back to the door.

"Mister," Wade said presently, "suppose you show me your bill o' sale or whatever else y' got t' prove you own this place."

Marshall rubbed his chin reflectively. He raised his head suddenly. His jaw hung for a moment; then he snapped it shut.

"I'll be doggoned!" he said like a man making a sudden and unhappy discovery. "I'll be a lop-eared son-uva-gun if I even thought o' askin' fer anything beside a key t' th' place! How d'you like that?"

Wade's lips tightened. His right arm jerked clumsily and his gun cleared its holster. But before the big man could snap it upward, a big Colt flashed into Marshall's hand and thundered deafeningly. Wade dropped his gun hastily, made a convulsive grab with his left hand and clutched his right wrist tightly. He glowered at Marshall, who was grim and steely-eyed now.

"Awright!" Marshall said through his teeth. "You near th' door! Reach fer th' ceilin' or I'll blast you apart!"

The man scowled darkly, but when Marshall's Colt swung toward him in an encompassing circle, his hands climbed upward without further delay.

"An' keep 'em up there, too!" Marshall commanded. He swung himself over the counter. Wade, tight-lipped, and still gripping his shattered wrist, glared at him. However, he backed away a bit, watching Marshall warily but making every effort to keep a respectable distance from him. Marshall looked at him.

"Wade," he said shortly, "I've just got this much t' say t' you an' I want you t' remember it 'cause it goes fer your brother, too. From now on stay th' hell outta here. That clear? Th' next time I see that pot-belly o' yourn comin' through that door, I'm gonna start fillin' it full o' lead."

He brushed past the big man, halted briefly to kick Wade's gun against the far wall, then he strode over to the door.

"You," he said curtly to the man with the upraised hands. "What's your handle?"

The man's lips tightened.

"Go t' hell!" he snarled.

Marshall struck him squarely in the face. He reeled drunkenly, fell to his hands and knees.

"Get up!"

Slowly the man came erect again. Blood trickled out of a corner of his mouth.

"Wa-al?" Marshall demanded ruthlessly.

"It's Gort!"

"That's better. Next time don't be so free sendin' other folks where you're headin' for!" Marshall said sharply. "G'wan, th' both o' you—get outta here an' stay out!"

Gort obeyed promptly. He backed out of the bank, his hands still high over his head, lowering them only when he reached the curb. Wade turned slowly, looked at Marshall and at his gun that lay against the wall. Marshall shook his head significantly and the big man lumbered out. Marshall watched them mount, saw Wade ride away. Gort twisted around in the saddle and motioned vigorously; then suddenly he spurred his horse and dashed off. Marshall whirled, racked back to the counter and threw himself over it. There was a sudden pounding of hoofs, then an earsplitting thunder of guns. The windows fell in with a deafening crash.

Now, rifle in hand, Marshall arose and came racing out of the bank. He skidded to a stumbling stop at the curb, and half raised his rifle. The last horseman in line, twisting around in his saddle, his gun upraised, caught sight of him and leveled his gun. Marshall's rifle snapped upward; he fired twice.

The horseman stiffened, dropped his gun into the gutter. He turned slowly and toppled out of the saddle. He fell heavily, landed on his shoulder and crashed over limply on his face.

CHAPTER THREE
RAINBOW

THE NEXT morning there was a curious and sudden bustle of activity in Rainbow. There was a constant and noisy clatter of hoofs and a squeaking of wagon wheels and brakes as the townspeople returned to their homes and stores. Marshall, standing in the open doorway of the bank, watched them interestedly. He heard a step behind him and turned his head.

"Good morning," Fran said.

"Mornin'," he replied. He moved a bit, made room for her in the doorway. "Looks like a p'rade."

"Yes," she said soberly. "However, it isn't the first return of Rainbow's citizens that I've witnessed. The chances are this won't be the last."

He made no reply. They were silent for a moment, their eyes on the strange cavalcade that rumbled past them. Both looked up when a small wagon with a canvas top came abreast of the bank. The man and the woman on the driver's seat waved as they clattered by.

"Ben West and his wife," Fran said. "They run the hotel down the street."

Now a big man on an equally big horse emerged from between two prairie schooners. The man looked over, caught Fran's eye, smiled, touched the wide brim of his hat, swung his horse into the curb and pulled up.

"Sure grow 'em big out here," Marshall remarked, eyeing the man. "Who's he?"

"Mike Gallo," Fran answered. "He owns the Star Cafe. It's across the street from the hotel."

Gallo dismounted. He brushed some dust from the front of his long black coat, gave his hat brim an adjusting tug, then came striding up to the doorway.

"Mornin', Miss Fran," he said. He smiled again, revealing small, white, even teeth that flashed all the more noticeably because of his dark skin.

"Good morning, Mike," Fran said. "You came back sooner than usual, didn't you?"

The big man laughed softly.

"Suppose so," he admitted a bit sheepishly. "Sorry I had t' run out on you, Fran, but you know how it is with me an' th' Wades. I owe th'm a heap an' I don't deny it. That's why when anythin' comes up b'tween them an' somebody else, I can't take sides against 'em. I'm willin' to admit that if it wasn't fer them an' fer th' bus'ness they bring into th' Star—wa-al, th' Star just wouldn't be what is t'day."

"Of course," Fran replied. Marshall detected a trace of cold scorn in her voice.

"But," Gallo continued, "long's nuthin' happened to you, an' you're awright, reckon I c'n breathe easier now. This th' feller who made th' Wades eat dirt?"

"This is Marshall."

The big man nodded to him.

"Glad t' know you," he said. "Glad t' know anybody who'll stand up t' th' Wades."

"You oughta try it y'self sometime," Marshall said quietly. "You're big enough."

Mike grinned sheepishly.

"Yeah, I supose so," he acknowledged. "Still, it allus seems like it takes a stranger t' show you how a thing like that c'n be done. Anyway, soon's I heard what happened, I hot-footed it back."

Marshall grunted.

"You an' a heap more."

"Uh-huh, on'y how they found out about it sure beats me," Gallo said.

"An' who brung you word?" Marshall asked.

The big man's teeth flashed again in a knowing smile.

"Oh, word gets aroun', y'know," he answered. "I've seen you somewheres, ain't I?"

"Could be. I've been places."

"Yeah, sure, an' I've heard your name b'fore, too. You couldn't be th' feller who turned Leadville an' Chenango an' a couple o' them other hell-holes inside out an' showed th' polecats there that th' law was boss—could you?"

"I was sheriff o' Leadville an' a couple o' other places," Marshall said quietly.

"Wa-al," Gallo said, nodding, "I sure wish you were th' law here, too. Rainbow might be worth livin' in then."

Marshall felt Fran's eyes on his face. But when he looked down at her, she quickly averted her eyes.

"If I c'n be uv any help, Marshall," Gallo said, "just you get word t' me."

"Think I'll need any?"

The big man's face grew grim.

"If I know th' Wades like I figger I do," he answered, "you'll need more'n just help from me."

"That so?"

Gallo nodded.

"Nobody c'n ever kick them aroun' an' get away with it. Mebbe you're th' exception. But till you prove it to th'm, they'll do everythin' they c'n t' get you. 'Course, that's just th' way I got th'm figgered out. I'm willin' to admit they ain't monkeyed aroun' with a real gun thrower b'fore, an' that you're li'ble t' pin their ears back like all get-out. But all th' same, Mister, if I was you, I'd sure take it easy an' I'd sure watch my step."

"Thanks," Marshall said. "I'll bear that in mind."

Gallo nodded.

"Wa-al, I better get goin' again. Got t' get things organized fer bus'ness, y'know. Even one day makes a heap uva diff'rence. Be seein' you, Mrshall. You, too, Fran."

He turned on his heel and retraced his steps to the curb, mounted his horse and rode slowly up the street. Fran turned and went inside; Marshall followed her. He closed the door behind him with a backward thrust of his left leg. Fran halted, turned and looked up at him.

"Marshall—" she began.

He looked down at her, hooked his thumbs in his gun belt.

"Yeah?"

"You've been wonderfully kind to me," she said, "and brave. But I want you to leave Rainbow."

He grinned easily, boyishly.

"Tired o' havin' me aroun' a'ready?"

"No," she said gravely.

" 'Fraid th' Wades'll do things t' me?"

"They're too many for one man to stand off. It isn't fair to you and I don't want anything to happen to you. The bank isn't worth your life and I won't stand by and let you risk your life for it," she concluded.

"I've fought against bigger odds an' fer things that weren't half as important," he answered.

"I want you to leave Rainbow," she repeated. "Today. Now."

"An' if I don't?"

"Please . . . ."

He shook his head.

"Ferget about th' bank an' everything else, Fran. I'm stayin' on in Rainbow b'cause I want to. It's my job an' that's that."

"I—I don't understand."

"Suppose you don't try to, huh?"

"Then you won't go?"

He shook his head again.

"No," he said with finality. "If I work fer you, swell. If I don't, I'll just hafta go find me somethin' else t' do t' keep me here."

Marshall rode slowly out of town. Minutes later as he topped a rise he twisted around in the saddle and looked back. Below him he could see Rainbow and its busy street. He settled himself in the saddle again, and nudged the black with his knees. The big horse loped away, presently quickened his pace and broke into a swift, free-striding run. They swept over the ground in an easterly direction. A rifle cracked suddenly, spitefully, and Marshall threw himself forward instinctively against the black's neck. A bullet whined by overhead, spent itself in flight. The big horse whinnied nervously, excitedly. Marshall dug his spurs into the black's flanks, swerved him and sent him thundering away.

The rifle roared a second time and the bullet ploughed the earth a dozen feet ahead of them. Again Marshall swerved the plunging horse, whirled him around when they came abreast of a huge boulder, and pulled up behind it. Cautiously Marshall peered out over the sun-scorched top of the boulder. He spotted a tiny wisp of gunsmoke rising gently above a distant clump of brush.

"Awright, Mister," he gritted. "Long's I know where you're at, reckon it's up t' me t' do somethin' about it."

He backed the black away from the boulder.

"Awright," he said simply. "Let's go!"

He spurred the big horse, sent him flashing away; then suddenly he came circling back in a furious clatter of hoofbeats. Twenty feet from the brush he slowed the black, slid out of the saddle and jerked out a big Colt. The black whirled and raced away again.

Marshall raced forward. He fired twice into the brush, side-stepped nimbly to avoid presenting a stationary target for the hidden rifleman, swerved this way, then that, panting to an abrupt halt when there was a sudden stirring behind the brush. A horseman bent low over his mount's neck came plunging out of the brush.

"Why, you lousy—!" Marshall yelled.

His Colt thundered protestingly and the horse cried out, stumbled and tripped, hurling his rider over his head. The man struck the ground heavily, evidence that he was unprepared for the fall. He landed on his shoulder and crashed over in a limp, awkward heap of arms and legs. The wounded horse scrambled to his feet, wheeled and jogged away. Marshall, his gun raised and ready for another shot, burst through the brush. He jerked to a stumbling stop.

"Awright, you polecat!" he commanded. "Get up on your hind legs an' reach fer th' sky!"

There was no movement by the outstretched man, no response. Marshall eyed him warily for a moment; then, with his Colt leveled, he trudged forward, came up directly behind him. "Awright!" he said again. "Get up!"

Still there was no movement, no acknowledgment of Marshall's command. He frowned, and looked about him quickly, guardedly; when he spied the man's rifle lying on the ground a short distance away, he was satisfied. He holstered his gun, bent over the man, turned him over on his back. Marshall's eyes widened. He stared hard. Peeping out from beneath the man's hat brim were blonde curls. He gulped and swallowed, stared hard at a tiny thread of blood that suddenly appeared between the curls and worked its way downward, halting when it reached a curving eyebrow.

"Holy cow!" he muttered. "A girl!"

He whipped out his bandana, knelt down beside her and gently wiped away the blood. The black came up behind him, nudged him, and Marshall looked up. He pocketed his handkerchief, hitched up his pants and bent over the girl again, swept her up into his arms and turned to the black.

"Steady," he said, and got to his feet. He lifted the unconscious girl into the saddle, steadied her with one hand, gripped the reins and swung up behind her. She sank back against him. "Awright."

The black turned his head and looked at the girl. He whinnied softly and Marshall nudged him with his knees.

"Go 'head," he commanded.

Slowly they retraced their steps; half an hour later they clattered into Rainbow. There were people on the street, and they halted their conversations or activities and eyed him interestedly. Mike Gallo was standing in the open doorway of his place. He looked up.

"Marshall!" he called. He came striding to the curb. Marshall pulled up.

"Know her?" he asked, nodding toward the limp figure that lay against his chest.

Gallo looked at her sharply. His eyes widened.

"Hey!" he said quickly. "What happened t' her?"

"Know 'er?" Marshall repeated.

"Sure," Gallo answered.

"Awright then. Who is she?"

"Eadie Wade."

Marshall's eyebrows arched.

"Oh, yeah?"

Gallo nodded vigorously.

"Oh, yeah, is right. Mister, you got y'self a heap o' trouble on your hands now if you had anything t' do with whatever happened t' her."

"That so? Th' Wades use her in their bus'ness?"

Gallo's face darkened.

"Look, Marshall—do me a favor an' y'self. Lemme have Eadie an' you get th' hell outta Rainbow fast's that horse o' yourn c'n carry you."

"No, thanks. I'll hang on to 'er fer now anyway."

Marshall nudged the black, and the big horse clattered away. In another minute they halted again, this time in front of the bank. Marshall slipped out of the saddle. Gently he lowered the girl, settled her in his arms, turned and trudged across the sidewalk. The door opened and Fran appeared. Marshall grinned at her.

"Brung you a boarder," he said lightly. "Know 'er?"

Fran held the door wide. Marshall halted on the threshhold. Fran peered hard at the Wade girl.

"Why, that's Edith Wade," she said quickly.

"That's what Gallo said."

"But—"

"She took a nasty spill offa her horse," Marshall said. "I'll tell 'bout it later on. Right now th' best thing we c'n do fer 'er is t' get 'er t' bed."

Fran turned without a word. Marshall, shifting the unconscious girl in his arms, followed at Fran's heels. They went through a door at the very rear of the bank, down a narrow length of hallway, then into a small room at the far end of it. Fran turned to him.

"Put her down on the bed," she said.

Marshall obeyed. Fran pushed past him and bent over the girl.

"Edith!" she said.

When there was no response, she went swiftly to a washstand in the corner of the room. She opened a drawer, whipped out a towel, dipped one end of it into the water, turned and came back to the bed. Again she bent over the Wade girl. Gently she bathed her face and wrists. Half a dozen times she came erect, went back to the water basin and dampened the towel; it was probably fifteen minutes later when Edith Wade stirred.

"Thank goodness!" Fran said. She put down the towel, seated herself on the edge of the bed, took Edith's hands in hers. "Edith!"

The girl's eyelids flickered, and presently her eyes opened.

"Feel better now?" Fran asked.

Edith's eyes ranged past her. She looked at Marshall for a moment, flushed suddenly and hastily, awkwardly, then averted her eyes. Marshall, watching her, frowned. He straightened up, hitched up his belt, shifted his holsters a bit.

"Don't suppose you need me in here any more," he said. He turned, trudged to the door, halted in the doorway and looked back. "Fran."

She turned and looked at him.

"You better tell 'er that she's damned lucky t' be where she is right now 'stead o' out in th' brush with a bullet in 'er," he said coldly. There was anger in his voice and eyes. "Folks who go 'round takin' pot shots at other folks are doggoned lucky when they don't get plugged instead. If she aims t' stay alive, she better not push 'er luck too far. There's a limit t' everything, 'specially luck."

He jerked at his hat brim viciously.

"There's another thing you might tell 'er, too," he added presently. Fran looked at him quietly, patiently. "Tell 'er t' leave killin's to 'er brothers. They're supposed t' be good at th'm, 'specially when th' other feller ain't lookin'. As fer her, she can't shoot straight, even when she's got a bead on a feller."

He stormed out and pulled the door shut behind him. He was tight-lipped when he came out of the bank. Mike Gallo, sober-faced, came striding up to him. Marshall's frown reflected his annoyance with the man.

"Oh," he grunted. "So it's you again, eh?"

"She awright?" Gallo asked anxiously.

"Who's she?"

"Eadie, o' course. Who d'you think I'm askin' about?"

"Oh, her," Marshall grunted. "Yeah, she's awright. Got 'erself a bump on 'er head, but that's about all. How come you're so all-fired worried about 'er?"

"I'm on'y thinkin' o' you," Gallo answered.

Marshall's lip curled.

"Don't bother y'self about me, Mister," he said coldly. "I don't need 'nybody t' ride herd over me, leastways not yet, anyway. An' when I do, depend on it, I won't ask you t' do it."

Gallo shrugged a thick shoulder.

"Awright," he said with finality. "If that's th' way you feel about it, reckon it's awright with me. Eadie ready t' go home yet?"

Marshall's lips thinned into a straight line.

"No!" he snapped. "But when she is, I'll see to it that she gets there awright. I'm still able t' get about by m'self; so's my horse. Between us we'll handle her awright."

Gallo eyed him for a moment, then he smiled.

" 'Course," he said. "So long."

He turned and marched off. Marshall followed him with his eyes until the big man turned into the Star Cafe.

"I don't like that feller," he said half aloud. "Some day he's gonna get under my feet an' I'm just natur'lly gonna walk all over 'im!"

CHAPTER FOUR

THE STRANGE COMPANIONS

IT WAS evening when Marshall and Edith Wade—both of them sitting awkwardly and stiffly erect astride the big black—rode slowly eastward over the night-darkened range.

From time to time the black turned his head and looked up at them curiously, seemingly unable to understand the silence between them. He whinnied once or twice, hopefully, but when there was no acknowledgment or response from Marshall, not even his usual reassuring pat on the black's neck, the big horse lapsed into silence too. The range was quiet, its heavy silence pierced only occasionally by the creaking of the saddle or the stirrups.

It was now more than an hour since they had left Rainbow, yet in all that time neither of them had uttered a single word. Each sat stiffly erect to avoid touching the other, an exacting if not a difficult feat for two people astride the same horse. A chill wind swept over them suddenly, and the girl in her cotton dress and equally lightweight jacket that Fran had insisted upon her taking reacted to it instantly. She bowed her head and drew in her arms close against her body.

"Want my blanket aroun' you?" Marshall asked.

"No!" she answered without raising her head.

"Ain't any sense freezin', y'know," he continued calmly. "Not when you don't hafta."

"I'm quite warm, thank you," she said stiffly.

"Awright," he said with an unconscious shrug of his shoulder. "Suit y'self."

He leaned forward suddenly and snapped her jacket collar upward to shield her neck. She did not remonstrate with him this time; neither did she voice an objection. The wind swirled about for another minute; then just as suddenly as it had burst upon them, it raced away into the night. Edith raised her head, and relaxed a bit with an audible sigh. The black stumbled over a half-buried rock, tripped clumsily and went down to his knees. Marshall's arm shot out instantly and gripped the girl securely for a moment, but only for that moment. She clutched the saddlehorn frantically. The black came erect again in that brief space of time and the girl pushed Marshall's arm away.

"I was on'y tryn' t' save you from takin' another spill," he said coldly. "But don't worry. I won't bother m'self again, not even if it looks like you're gonna break your neck!"

She did not reply. He moved back a bit in the saddle, tightened his grip on the reins.

"Stubborn an' nasty an' plumb ornery," he muttered half aloud. "I'm doggoned sorry I didn't stay put an' let you go home by yourself."

"Why didn't you?" she demanded.

"Because I'm just a danged fool!" he said loudly.

"That's quite evident," she said curtly.

His lips tightened. The moon disappeared now behind a cloud and the hushed range was frighteningly dark. Fantastically formed shadows darted here and there. Some of them seemed to arise directly in their path, flitted past them so closely that once or twice the black cried out and jerked to an abrupt halt that almost jolted the girl out of the saddle. Marshall made no attempt to help her. He sat perfectly still and waited for her to steady herself; then he made the black go on again. The wind returned presently, and dust and vagrant leaves swirled about them wildly. Marshall glanced skyward.

"Storm comin'," he told himself. He nudged the big horse with his knees. "Go on."

The black quickened his pace, but there was no lessening of the wind nor eluding it. It hovered over them persistently. Marshal whipped up his own jacket collar. He halted the black and dismounted, unstrapped his blanket and swung up again into the saddle. Without a word he opened the blanket and draped it over the girl's shoulders.

"Awright," he said to the black. "Go 'head!"

Through the dark night they rode, a mile, then another, until finally the storm broke upon them. It was a light but cold drizzle at first, then a heavier rain and finally a furious, drenching downpour.

"Hey!" he yelled, and nudged the girl. "Know o' any place aroun' here where we c'n get shelter?"

She turned her head.

"We should be near an old line-rider's shack," she replied.

"Yeah? How near?"

"Oh, it can't be very far now."

He spurred the black and the big horse broke into a swift gallop.

"There it is!" the girl cried suddenly.

She pushed the blanket away and pointed, and Marshall's eyes followed her finger. He jerked the reins, swerved the black; in another minute they pulled up in front of a darkened shack. Marshall slid out of the saddle. He turned and held out his arms to the girl.

"Come on," he said briefly.

When she seemed to hesitate, he stepped closer and whipped away the blanket and lifted her out of the saddle and put her down on the wet ground. He turned on his heel and went swiftly to the shack door. He tried the knob; when it failed to open he muttered something under his breath, stepped back and crashed into the door. It flew open, collided with something inside the shack. He stepped over the threshold and disappeared in the darkness.

"Awright!" she heard him call presently. "You c'n come in now!"

She halted again in the open doorway. Suddenly a tiny yellow light flared and flamed. There was a crude, makeshift table in the middle of the shack. Marshall, a lighted match in one hand, was bent over a lamp that stood atop the table. The lamp flamed with a dazzling brightness.

"Swell," he said, and straightened up.

He hitched up his gun belt and strode past her, went outside again. She heard his voice, heard the horse whinny. It was several minutes later when Marshall returned. He closed the door with a backward thrust of his foot and handed her the blanket.

"Use it," he said. "It ain't wet all th' way through."

He brushed past her again. There were several upended boxes in a far corner of the shack and he brought one forward, placed it near the table.

"Sit down," he said, and turned away again.

He was hunting for something now. She followed him with her eyes, and finally saw him hold up an empty pail. He smashed a couple of the boxes with the butt of a big Colt, broke the wood across his knee and filled the pail with it. He struck another match, placed the pail close by on the floor, stepped back and leaned against the far wall. Soon a flame crackled in the pail and he nodded to himself.

"Reckon that's about all I c'n do fer you t'night," he said, turning toward her. "Sorry I can't rustle up some grub, or at least some hot coffee. You'll just hafta do without it till you get home again."

She sat down on the box and draped the blanket around her. He placed another of the boxes against the wall for himself and seated himself upon it. They were silent again, their eyes focused on the bright, warming fire in the pail. The rain thudded on the roof, beat against the walls and the door. The girl drew the blanket closer. Presently she closed her eyes.

It was early the next morning—a clear, warm, sunny morning—when Marshall rode slowly into Rainbow and pulled up in front of the bank. He swung himself out of the saddle, turned his head when he heard the door open. Fran was framed in the doorway.

"Hi!" he called cheerily.

"Hi, yourself!" she replied.

He came striding up to the door, while her eyes ranged over him, probed his face.

"What's th' matter?" he asked, halting in front of her. He pushed his hat back from his eyes and hooked his thumbs in his belt. "Your eyes are red. You been cryin' or somethin'?"

She shook her head and smiled fleetingly.

"I didn't sleep very well," she answered, and quickly averted her eyes.

"Oh," he said. He looked at her sharply. "What kept you awake? Worryin' 'bout me an' why I didn't get back?"

"Of course not! You're free to come and go as you please. Besides that, you're a full-grown man."

"Uh-huh, on'y you were worried, weren't you?"

"We-ll, when it got to be midnight—"

"You had it all figgered out that th' Wades'd finished me off. Fact o' th' matter is, Fran, I didn't see either o' th'm or any o' their hired hands. When we reached th' Bar-O it was just after sunup and—"

She looked up at him quickly.

"Sunup?" she repeated.

"Uh-huh. When that storm busted loose on us, we hadda find some place t' duck into, an' lucky fer us we run into some ol' line-rider's shack an' spent th' night there. Good thing Eadie knew where it was. I'da never found it by myself in all that storm an' darkness. Anyway, th' storm let up somewheres b'fore dawn an' we got goin' again. When we hit th' Bar-O—"

"I don't suppose you've had any breakfast," Fran interrupted. "The coffee's still hot and you'll find muffins in the bread-box. Do you mind helping yourself while I attend to some other things?"

She turned on her heel and went back inside. He stared at her for a moment, followed her slim, swiftwalking figure with his puzzled eyes until she disappeared from sight. He rubbed his chin thoughtfully.

"Now what d'you suppose got into her?" he muttered. "Just get started tellin' 'er 'bout last night an' she plumb freezes up an' hightails it."

He heard an approaching step on the sidewalk behind him, and turned as old Tom came across the street.

"Mornin', ol'-timer," Marshall said.

The old man halted beside him.

"Mornin'. Fran know you're back?"

"Yeah, sure. I was just talkin' to 'er."

"She was sure worried 'bout you last night. Wouldn't turn in, no matter what I tol' 'er. She just kept pacin' up an' down, turnin' first t' th' window an' listenin' there fer a spell, then openin' th' door an' peerin' out. Fin'lly—oh, reckon it was somewheres 'round three o'clock—she sat down near th' window an' dozed off."

"Heck, there wasn't any call fer any o' that! I've been out all night b'fore. B'sides, I c'n take care 'o myself, b'lieve me."

"Yeah, I suppose you c'n. But women c'n get th' dangedest funniest ideas, y'know, an' when they do, they c'n build 'em up till they almost lose 'em in th' clouds."

"So I've heard tell," Marshall commented.

"B'sides—" the old man continued, then paused abruptly.

"Yeah? What were you gonna say?"

"Marshall, somethin' tells me that Fran's taken more'n just a shine to you. Y'know, when a girl starts stayin' up nights worryin' 'bout a feller, an' when she walks aroun' th' house not seein' where she's goin'—brother, she's—"

"Hold it, partner," Marshall said quickly. "Ain't you readin' th' signs all wrong?"

Tom grinned toothlessly.

"Mister, I've had six sisters an' all o' th'm got th'mselves husbands. B'sides that, I've had two wives in my time, so doggone it, I oughta know what they're up to when I see 'em moonin' around like Fran's been doin'. All I gotta say t' you is this—if you ain't th' marryin' kind, partner, I'd kinda s'ggest that you climb back up on that horse o' yourn an' start goin' places, but fast!"

Marshall sauntered into the Star Cafe, halted when he came to the bar and leaned on it. Mike Gallo came along presently and stopped beside him.

"Evenin', Marshall."

"Oh, hello."

The big man turned his head for a moment and looked anxiously toward the door.

"S'matter?" Marshall asked, watching him.

Gallo turned to him. His face was grim.

"I understan' th' sheriff's moseyin' aroun' town with a couple o' his deputies an' that they're kinda anxious t' meet up with you," he said in a low voice.

Marshall's eyebrows arched.

"That so?"

"Yeah."

"An' what d'they wanna talk t' me about?"

"Th' warrant th' sheriff's totin' aroun' says t' lock you up fer murder."

"That's mighty interestin'. Who's th' late lamented?" Marshall asked.

A bartender, a short, pudgy man with a glistening bald head, a much too long and soiled apron tied around his waist and a damp, soggy towel slung over his arm appeared behind the bar. He eyed Marshall.

"Awright, Mister," he said after a moment's patient wait. "What'll it be?"

Gallo gave him an icy stare.

"Beat it," he said curtly. "We're talkin'."

"Y'mean you are," Marshall said quickly. "An' since I'm doin' th' listenin', reckon I c'n handle a drink at th' same time. Whiskey, bartender."

The latter shrugged. Finally he placed a half-filled, uncorked bottle in front of Marshall, followed it with a glass; then after a moment's hesitation he placed another glass on the bar at Gallo's elbow. Marshall poured himself a drink and turned to Gallo.

"How 'bout you?" he asked.

Gallo shook his head and Marshall grinned lightly.

"It's your own stuff," he said dryly. "You oughta know better'n anybody else if it's worth drinkin'."

"Oh, it's awright," the big man said quickly. "It's—it's just that I ain't drinkin'."

Marshall lifted his glass, drained it at a swallow... Gallo's hand shot out, gripped Marshall's arm.

"Hodges!" he said out of a corner of his mouth. "Watch yourself!"

He straightened up, patted Marshall on the back and turned away.

"Be seein' you," he called lightly over his shoulder.

Marshall turned quickly.

"Hey!" he called loudly. "Who was that polecat I'm supposed to've killed off?"

"Curly Bendix," a surly voice said behind him. The muzzle of a gun collided with his spine and he stiffened. "Put down that glass, Mister, an' turn aroun' with your hands high!"

CHAPTER FIVE

THE TRICKS OF THE TRADE

MARSHALL, his hands half raised, turned slowly. In front of him stood a bulky, scowling man whose leveled gun gaped at Marshall's chest; behind him were his deputies, two men with silver stars pinned to their shirt fronts who eyed Marshall interestedly.

"You're under arrest fer th' murder o' Curly Bendix," Sheriff Hodges said briefly.

Marshall smiled coldly.

"Never heard o' him," he said calmly. "Who dreamed him up? Th' Wades?"

Hodges bristled with a great show of indignation.

"Nob'dy dreamed him up!" he retorted angrily. "Nobody had to! He was real, awright, an' plenty healthy too, leastways till you plugged him. As fer th' Wades, they had nuthin' t' do with this a-tall. Runnin' you down was my idea, see?"

"If you say so."

"Awright then!" the sheriff sputtered. "I'm th' law in Rainbow an' nobody else. Get that straight!"

"It's awright with me. I suppose you got yourself fixed up with a warrant an' that it's all legal-like like th' law says it has t' be?"

Sheriff Hodges grinned, then laughed heartily.

"Oh, sure!"

"Reckon then you won't mind showin' me th' warrant?"

Hodges' eyes glinted, belying his laugh.

" 'Course not!" he answered readily. His thick fingers tightened around the butt of his gun. "Take a good look at it, Mister. It's starin' straight at you. Th' gov'nor, th' supreme court an' everythin' else all rolled up into one Colt!"

Marshall did not reply.

"Take his guns, Boys!" Hodges commanded. His two deputies looked at him, then at Marshall. "Go 'head, Pete, Sully!"

The man named Pete hitched up his pants and came forward, while Sully contented himself by simply moving closer to Marshall, but made no attempt to assist his mate in disarming the black-clad man. Pete halted directly in front of Marshall and reached for the latter's gun butts. Marshall grabbed him suddenly. Pete was taken completely by surprise; hence he offered no resistance. With a mighty surge of strength Marshall hurled him away, sent him plunging wildly toward Hodges. Sully, wide-eyed and open-mouthed, stepped forward. Pete came careening into him and both collided heavily and stumbled backward, trampling the equally unprepared and surprised Hodges. The sheriff, kicked painfully by one man and trampled on by the other, cried out, and when an elbow was driven into the pit of his ample stomach, he gasped and dropped his gun. Pete, stumbling awkwardly when Hodges shoved him away, bent down to pick up the gun; instead he kicked it away.

"Doggone you, Pete!" Hodges bellowed. "Doggone your clumsy hide! I oughta—!"

"Hold it!" Marshall snapped. "Come on, th' three o' you—hoist 'em an' hoist 'em high!"

The lawmen turned and stared hard. There was a big black Colt in Marshall's right hand and the muzzle yawned at them hungrily and ominously. Slowly their hands climbed upward. Hodges, red-faced, was panting; his deputies were equally red-faced and both appeared dazed by what had happened. Marshall's lip curled scornfully.

"You're a fine c'llection o' lawmen, awright," he said coldly. "Th' three o' you couldn't catch a cold."

Hodges shifted his bulk from one leg to the other.

"You," Marshall said, looking squarely at the sheriff. "This Bendix maverick I'm accused o' killin'—who was he?"

The sheriff scowled.

"One o' th' Wades' riders," he grumbled.

"Uh-huh. An' where was I supposed to've killed 'im?"

"Right down th' street."

Marshall looked up quickly.

"Oh, I think I get it now," he said. "I remember some feller on a horse—it was after I threw Wade an' Gore outta th' bank—anyway, this feller was ridin' down th' street. He turned aroun' and threw down on me, on'y I shot first. So that was th' Curly Bendix you've been yappin' about—right?"

Hodges averted his eyes.

"Yeah," he mumbled. "On'y that ain't th' way I heard it told."

"Mebbe not, but that's th' way it happened."

Hodges mumbled again, indistinctly, and Marshall glared at him. The big Colt came up a bit higher.

"You fellers get th' hell outta here," Marshall said gruffly. "What's more, if you aim t' go on livin', take a tip from me an' steer clear o' me. I'm liable t' ferget myself next time I run into you an' start blastin' away 'stead o' feelin' sorry for you. G'wan—get goin'."

Hodges turned slowly, and Pete bumped into him. When the sheriff jerked around and glared at him, Pete backed away hastily. Slowly and carefully, giving one another ample room so as to avoid further crowding and trampling, the trio filed out of the place. Marshall turned, halted when he spied Hodges' gun lying just beyond him, strode over to it, edged it away from the bar, drew back his foot and kicked viciously. The gun, caught squarely by Marshall's booted toe, spun toward the open doorway. It sailed over the threshold, rose just a bit higher as it cleared the narrow sidewalk, then dipped sharply and dropped limply into the gutter.

Marshall holstered his gun. Mike Gallo tapped him on the shoulder.

"Say," Mike said with a relaxed grin. "That was awright th' way you handled them three fellers. You made 'em look silly."

"There are tricks in every trade," Marshall answered. Even in how t' arrest a feller an' get away with it."

"Yeah, I suppose that's so," Gallo acknowledged. He grinned again and looked toward the bar. "Think I c'n stand a drink now. How 'bout joinin' me?"

"Awright."

They leaned over the bar; presently the pudgy man appeared.

"Drinkin', Gents?" he asked.

Gallo scowled darkly.

"Yeah," he snapped. "On'y none o' that belly wash this time. Trot out some o' my special stuff."

The bartender looked at him questioningly.

"Huh? Where d'you keep it, Boss?"

"Don't gimme any o' that innocent stuff," Gallo said gruffly. "You know well's I do where th' stuff is. You've had more uv it 'n I have."

"Aw, now, wait a minute, Boss . . . ."

"You heard me! Seems like every time I turn my back, you're gone. Th' next time I see you, you're comin' outta th' back room. No wonder th' stuff's dwindlin' so fast. G'wan—go get us a bottle uv it an' no back talk!"

Marshall strode briskly along the darkened street toward the bank. Suddenly a shot rang out, and he froze in his tracks, his hands dangling crablike just above the jutting butts of his guns. A man with a Colt clutched in his upraised hand staggered drunkenly out of a nearby alley. Marshall eyed him carefully. When the man came abreast of him, he fired again, skyward.

"H'ray!" he yelled.

Marshall, turning, watched the man for another minute, then went on again. The man halted, straightened up, wheeled and leveled his gun and fired. The bullet whined past Marshall's head, and he whirled around instantly, crouching, a readied Colt gripped tightly in his hand. The man who had fired at him wheeled like a flash and fled. He swerved suddenly and plunged into a darkened alley and disappeared. Marshall dashed after him, came thundering up to the entrance to the alley, and skidded to a stop. He shook his head. Pursuit, he realized, would be nothing more than wasted effort. The man, he decided, had doubtless planned his escape route beforehand, and now, in the darkness and in the depths of unfamiliar alleys, he would easily outdistance Marshall. The latter holstered his gun.

"Damn," he muttered. "I'd sure like t' have caught up with that polecat. I'da kicked 'is teeth out!"

He turned on his heel and trudged away.

"Reckon I'd better start gettin' used t' havin' fellers take pot shots at me," he muttered presently. "Th' Wades will try every trick in th' book an' then some t' get me."

He hitched up his belt.

"I'll just have t' keep one step ahead o' th'm," he concluded with finality.

He gave his gun belt another hitching-up, and glanced across the street. A store directly opposite was suddenly plunged into darkness. As he moved alertly, a rifle cracked ominously. He threw himself sideways, and heard a bullet whine past, heard it splinter the framework of a door just behind him. His guns flashed into his hands and he plunged across the street. He thought he detected a shadowy movement somewhere within the store; as he came closer to it he saw that it was vacant. The indistinguishable shadow moved again and Marshall's guns leaped upward and flamed and belched with a. thunderous roar. A window fell in with a deafening, shattering crash. He headed for the door, planning to smash it in. Midway he swerved and dashed toward an alley that ran alongside. He came plunging into it, caught a fleeting glimpse of a shadowy, running figure at the far end of the alley and fired twice, two lightning shots that blended into a single ear-splitting report. The shadow stopped, dissolved into a man who staggered, tottered, gasped and suddenly crumpled up.

"Reckon that's what," Marshall said half aloud. "That kinda squares things between me an' th' Wades, leastways fer t'night, anyway. One feller got away an' one didn't. That makes it an even count an' I'm satisfied."

He shoved his guns into their holsters, turned and tramped across the street. A minute later he reached the bank, found the door unlocked and went in, bolting the door behind him. He heard a quick step and looked up. Fran was standing in the connecting doorway.

"Oh," he said lightly. "How come th' door wasn't locked? An' how come you ain't turned in yet?"

He came sauntering forward.

"I heard some shooting," she said quietly.

He grinned boyishly.

"Come t' think uv it," he replied, "I did, too."

"Did you do any of the shooting?"

He laughed softly.

"Some of it," he said casually. Her anxious eyes probed his face. "One feller put on like he was drunk, an' then when he got past me, th' son-uva-gun took a shot at me. He got away, run like a thief down some dark alley an' left me high an' dry."

"One fellow?" she echoed. "You mean there was a second attempt to shoot you, too?"

He nodded grimly.

"Yeah, right across th' street," he answered. "There was a feller with a rifle planted there in an empty store. He's ready fer a real plantin' now. I got him."

She was silent for a moment.

"Now don't you go worryin' about me," he said. "I c'n take care o' myself."

"Marshall," she began presently, "won't you please listen to reason and leave Rainbow while you can? While you're still able to?"

"You don't understand, Fran ...."

She gestured impatiently.

"I know, Marshall," she said quickly, interrupting him. "You've a job to do here."

"That's right."

"But what kind of a job is it that you must subject yourself to cowardly attacks?" she demanded. "I don't understand it."

"Look, Fran—suppose we just f'rget th' hull thing, huh? Nuthin's happened to me an' nuthin's goin' to."

She was momentarily silent, but after a brief minute she looked up at him again.

"Marshall—" she began.

"Yeah?"

"Marshall, if I offered to go with you, would you leave Rainbow?"

"Wa-al, now ...."

"Would you?" she asked again.

Their eyes met, and they looked at each other steadily, unwaveringly.

"You're a swell girl, Fran," he said slowly.

"You'll do it?"

He hitched up his belt again, drew a deep breath, faced her once more.

"No, Fran," he said quietly. "I wouldn't. I couldn't."

She turned and walked swiftly away.

CHAPTER SIX
THE BAR-O

Ed and Jim Wade sat quietly at the kitchen table as Edith finished drying the breakfast dishes. They followed her every move with their eyes, watched as she hung the wet towel on the bar above the sink, watched too as she put away the dishes.

"Eadie," Ed said finally, turning and looking at her, "I sure wish you'da plugged that feller Marshall when you had th' chance to."

"Me, too!" Jim said, and thumped the table with his big hand.

"If you'da got th' skunk," Ed continued, "we woulda been awright by now. We'da had our dough outta th' bank an' we'd be sittin' pretty."

Jim nodded vigorously.

"That's right," he said gravely. "We sure woulda!"

Ed turned his head and gave Jim a cold stare.

"You wanna tell this, or am I gonna?" he demanded. "Where was I?"

"You were talkin' about our dough."

"Oh, yeah! Y'know, Eadie, we had Fran right where we wanted 'er."

"Uh-huh," Jim said with another vigorous nod of his head. "She was plumb scared t' death. She was all set t' blab 'er guts out."

Ed glared at him and Jim wilted.

"Look, Jim," Ed said curtly. "There never was no story that needed two t' tell it. If you can't keep quiet till I'm done talkin', you go ahead an' tell it an' I'll shut up. But if I'm gonna tell it, you shut up an' stay shut!"

Jim averted his eyes and sank back in his chair.

"Thanks," Ed said with a grin. "Like I was gonna say, Eadie, Fran on'y needed one push outta us an' she'da led us right t' th' spot where 'er ol' man'd buried th' dough he stole from th' bank. But right then Marshall come along an' that was that. He saved Fran's hide an' th' dough, too."

Jim raised his head, and Ed looked at him questioningly.

" 'Smatter? I ferget somethin'?"

Jim shrugged.

"Don't ask me," he replied. "This is your story, ain't it?"

Ed scowled darkly, clamped his jaws shut and sat back in his chair. Jim laughed softly.

"What he's tryin' t' lead up to, Eadie," he said smoothly, "an' flounderin' aroun' like a drownin' steer instead, is that we ain't worryin' because our dough's gone. It's on account o' you an' your dough. Y'see, Eadie, we're men, an' men c'n allus get along, dough or no dough. But it's diff'rent, heaps diff'rent, believe me, an' tougher, too, when it happens t' be a girl who ain't got 'ny dough out here."

"Tough ain't half th' word fer it," Ed said curtly.

"You're both firmly convinced that Fran Grant not only knows that her father looted the bank," Eadie said, "but that she also knows where he buried the money. Aren't you?"

"I'll bet every buck I'll ever have," Ed said quickly, "against a button that she knows all there is t' know about it."

"If she don't know," Jim added, "then nobody does, an' that goes double fer 'er old man, th' polecat! An' if that's th' case, then our dough just sprouted wings an' flew outta th' bank an' disappeared ferever. Doggone it, Eadie, does that make sense t' you, or t' you, Ed?"

"No," Ed said flatly. "It don't!"

"How 'bout you, Eadie?"

"No," she answered doubtfully. "I don't suppose it does."

"Then there y'are!" Jim said triumphantly.

"There's just one more thing we want you t' know, Eadie," Ed began, and paused.

"Yes?"

"Eadie," Ed continued, "I think you know how you stand with Jim an' me. You gotta admit we've never treated you like a step-sister, have we? We've allus acted like you was one o' us an' nuthin' else but. Awright then. If we felt diff'rent about you, believe me, 'stead o' worryin' about you an' about you losin' th' last buck you got in th' world, we'd prob'bly say, heck, it's tough, an' then we'd just ferget about it."

"That's right!" Jim said with a nod. "But because we're just one fam'ly, we gotta stick t'gether an' do somethin'. Eadie, you're in this same's we are. We're countin' on you doin' your part."

" 'Course she will!" Ed said heartily. "Eadie's a Wade clear through an' that means she'll see this thing right down t' th' end no matter what happens. Blood's thicker'n water, y'know, an' that's what counts!"

"Good," Jim said. "Ed, this Marshall feller's in th' way. We gotta do somethin' about him."

"Awright. You got some plan in mind?"

"I'm workin' on one right now. But there'll be parts in it fer all three o' us."

"I wouldn't want it no other way. Th' Wades'll go in on it all t'gether or they'll stay out uv it. You go ahead an' work it out, Jim, an' when it's ready, just you say th' word an' tell each uv us what we gotta do an' we'll do it. That's th' way you want it, Eadie, ain't it?"

She moistened her lips with a quick, darting movement of her tongue, and nodded mutely. Then she turned suddenly and went out of the room. Jim and Ed sat back quietly. They heard her quick, light tread on the stairs; presently they heard a door on the upper floor open, then close. Jim relaxed, grinned and nudged his brother.

"How'd we do?" he asked. "Fer my money we put it over."

Ed shrugged his shoulders.

"I hope so," he replied. "From th' looks o' things, we're gonna have our work cut out fer us handlin' this Marshall feller an'—"

"Wait a minute," Jim interrupted. "I know that Johnny Farrell got a shot at Marshall last night an' missed, but what about Joe Tyler?"

"He ain't back yet."

"Wa-al, then we've still got a chance, ain't we? Joe's a damned good man with a rifle, an' mebbe he got Marshall."

"Mebbe, but th' fact that he ain't back yet makes me figger that he didn't do any better'n Farrell did. You know danged well, Jim, that if he plugged Marshall fer keeps, he'da hightailed it out here right off."

"Yeah," Jim admitted. "I suppose he woulda, an' if he couldn't make it, then he'da managed somehow t' get word uv it t' us so's we'd know."

"Uh huh. Jim, fer all we know, mebbe Marshall got Tyler instead o' th' other way around."

"Y'might have somethin' there, Ed. Then fer all we know, while we're chewin' th' rag here, waitin' fer Tyler t' show up, he might be layin' in some alley deader'n all hell!"

Ed nodded gravely.

"That's why I'm hopin' our story an' our little act we cooked up went over with Eadie," he concluded. "I gotta feeling that Marshall's too strong fer us t' handle 'less we get 'im when he ain't expectin' anything t' happen to 'im."

"Go on. I'm listenin'."

"Wa-al, what I'm figgerin' on is that we're gonna need Eadie t' help us get him. Once she's sold on th' idea that while he's helpin' Fran stand us off, he's actu'lly helpin' Fran cheat Eadie outta her dough, little Eadie is gonna act up like any other woman an' be willin' t' fix Marshall an' good. Hell, 'less I miss my guess, Jim, she might even play up t' Marshall, lead him off somewheres where we'll be layin' fer 'im an' then—"

Jim grinned broadly.

"That'll be th' end o' Mister Marshall!"

"Right!"

"Wa-al, supposin' that's th' way it works out, Ed. What about Eadie? Don't we hafta get rid o' her, too?"

"I got that figgered out, too."

Jim's eyes widened.

"Y'mean we're gonna—"

"No!" Ed said curtly. "After we kill off Marshall, th' rest'll be easy. We put some pressure on Fran, suddenly realize she don't know a danged thing about th' dough an' admit we got 'er wrong. 'Course it'll be tough on Eadie, so's t' make 'er feel better we'll suggest that we scrape up th' dough she needs t' take 'er back East...."

"Doggone it, that's just what she's allus wanted t' do!"

" 'Course it is! She goes back East an' outta our lives ferever an' we get her dough well's our own. That's th' hull story."

"You're awright, Ed! You're doggoned smart when it comes t' that kind o' thing!"

Ed smiled coldly.

"You don't know th' half uv it, Jim."

"Reckon that's right, too, Ed. But gettin' back t' cases—"

"Marshall's th' nut we gotta crack. Long's he lives we don't dare do a damned thing. That's why we gotta get things org'nized an' movin' toward gettin' rid o' him!"

It was an hour later when Ed Wade climbed the stairs to the upper floor and halted in front of Edith's room.

"Eadie!" he called.

There was no response.

"Eadie!" he called again after a brief wait. He heard a stirring, an indistinguishable movement behind the closed door, waited another moment, then rapped lightly. "Eadie!"

He heard a more distinct movement.

"She'll be answerin' now," he muttered to himself. "Probably been takin' a nap."

"Yes? What is it?"

"It's me, Eadie. Ed. I wanna see you a minute."

He heard a quick step, a key grated in the lock, then the door was opened.

"Hated t' bother you, Eadie," he said gently.

"Oh, that's all right!"

"Go take a look outta your window," he said, nodding toward it.

She eyed him questioningly, but when he waited patiently without offering to explain his request, she turned and went swiftly to the window at the far end of the room. She pushed the curtain aside and peered out, turned back suddenly, wide-eyed and white-faced.

"The men," she said quickly, breathlessly. "They're carrying someone into the bunkhouse!"

He nodded mutely. Then her eyes framed a question.

"Joe," he said simply. "Joe Tyler. He's dead. Sam Hodges just brung him here from town."

A gasp escaped her.

"I know how you feel about it," he said gently. "If I ain't mistaken, it was Joe who taught you how t' ride an' shoot. He was allus lookin' after you like he was your big brother. An' now—"

Her lips tightened.

"Who did it, Ed?" she demanded.

He moistened his lips with his tongue, withholding his reply purposely.

"Marshall?" she demanded.

He nodded, waited again.

"How—how did it happen?"

"Wa-al, seems like Marshall made some kinda crack about you," he answered slowly. " 'Course nobody could do anythin' like that in front o' Joe an' get away with it."

"Go on."

Ed drew a deep breath.

"Wa-al, I don't know much about what happened 'cept that Marshall managed t' get away from Joe, who went lookin' fer 'im. Seems kinda funny, leastways it does t' me, but when they found Joe he was layin' in 'n alley with two bullet holes in 'im."

She caught her lower lip between her teeth, stifling the gasp or perhaps a cry that arose in her throat.

"And Marshall?"

Ed's lips tightened, and his eyes grew steely.

"He got away with a hull skin. What I meant about it lookin' funny t' me was th' fact that when they come across Joe, he didn't even have a gun on 'im. I got an idea he was plugged somewheres else an' dragged into th' alley an' left there t' die. Chances are, Marshall musta give Joe th' slip, doubled back, come up behind 'im an' drilled 'im before Joe knew what was happenin'. Then there was one more thing—"

Her eyes clung to his face.

"Joe wasn't th' kind t' do 'is fightin' in no alley. He was th' kind that spoke his piece or did his fightin' right out in th' open. Th' hull damned thing smells t' me, an' from th' way I figger it out, Joe wasn't just shot. He was murdered in cold blood. An' Mister Marshall, th' dirty, lousy skunk, is gonna answer t' th' Wades fer that, believe me!"

He hitched up his belt viciously, turned and started toward the door, halted midway and turned around again.

"Y'know, Eadie," she heard him say, "I ain't th' kind who listens t' gossip an' such an' spreads it. But now that I think uv it, mebbe there is somethin' t' th' things I've been hearin'."

She turned quickly.

"What kind of things?"

"Oh, things 'bout Marshall—an' 'bout somebody else."

Her eyes probed his face, and he looked away, dug his boot toe into the faded carpet on the floor.

"You mean—"

"Th' hull town's buzzin' with stories 'bout th' goin's-on at th' bank," he blurted out, then looked up again defiantly. "Nob'dy c'n figger out why a feller like Marshall's stayin' around. He don't do anything that anybody c'n see. 'Less somebody's makin' his stayin' on in Rainbow mighty enticin', he shoulda been gone long ago."

She turned away from him slowly. He gave her a sidelong glance and went out of the room. Jim was waiting for him at the bottom of the stairs. Ed motioned to him to follow, led him through the kitchen and out of the house.

"Wa-al?"

Ed grinned evilly.

" 'Less I'm readin' th' signs wrong, she's just about ready t' slit Mister Marshall's throat fer 'im. I gave 'er a story that just about kicked th' props out from under 'er."

"An' she swallowed it?"

"Th' hull damned thing!"

Jim grinned back at him.

"Swell, Ed, swell!" he exulted; then he grew serious again. "Ed, I've been wonderin' about somethin'."

"Yeah—what?"

"Wa-al, Joe Tyler wasn't th' kind you could send off t' plug a feller in th' back. How come he agreed t' do it without kickin' up a fuss?"

"I told Joe somethin' that made him willin' t' do anything," Ed answered quietly.

Jim's eyes widened.

"What was that?" he asked.

"I tol' 'im that Marshall'd been makin' some nasty remarks about Eadie an' that was that. Joe didn't hafta hear no more. He grabbed 'is rifle, saddled up an' lit out fer Rainbow like a bat outta hell!"

CHAPTER SEVEN
RENDEZVOUS

THE BLACK came dashing into a boulder-rimmed circle, snorting protestingly when Marshall pulled him to a full stop. The clatter of approaching hoofs swelled. He had heard them earlier and he had instantly voiced a low-pitched, warning whinny; but instead of whirling him around and sending him racing away to a protected spot until the riders' identities could be determined, Marshall had simply patted the big horse's sleek neck and kept him on the trail. Now the black heard a hail. He turned his head and saw a cheery wave of a hand, saw Marshall acknowledge it and answer it. The newcomers broke into the circle and the black noticed that one of them was a woman. He bristled instantly. He disliked women, and his reason was simple and obvious: a fear that one of them would come between his master and himself. The black's fear mounted to a new height now; the woman was the prettiest he had ever seen. But in that same instant he recognized her. Her sorrel, a dainty-hoofed, clean-limbed mare, whinnied softly, musically, and the black eyed her interestedly. He felt Marshall swing himself out of the saddle; he saw him stride across the intervening space, hold out his arms and catch the woman in them as she slid to the ground. The black bristled again, but the mare sidled up to him and the big horse promptly forgot about his master and the woman.

The second rider was a lean, youthful man with a bandaged right arm in a sling. His horse, a big, powerful white animal, halted where directed, but made no attempt to join the other horses. The black turned his head once again, and saw Marshall clasp the woman in his arms, saw her raise her head, saw them cling tightly to each other in an embrace, then saw their lips meet. The man with the injured arm grinned down at them.

"Doggone!" he chuckled. "Must be th' air that does things like that t' folks! Go on, go on—don't pay any 'ttention t' me! I ain't important. I just come along fer th' ride!"

But now Marshall and the woman were walking over to him.

"How are you, Smith?" Marshall asked.

"Oh, so-so. You're lookin' fit, so I reckon things are shapin' up awright, eh?"

Marshall grinned up at him.

"Yeah, pretty good," he answered.

The horsemen nodded.

"How much longer d'you think it'll be?" he asked.

Marshall shrugged his shoulder.

"That's hard t' say, Smith. You oughta know how these things are. You can't push 'em. You hafta let 'em develop by th'mselves an' hope t' heck they won't take any longer'n they hafta."

"But, Ned—" the woman said, looking up at Marshall.

He smiled at her, put his arm around her waist.

"Now, honey, don't go gettin' impatient. You know I didn't wanna take this thing on. That feller made me do it," he said, nodding toward the man astride the white horse. "Y'know, it seems like I'm allus gettin' into messes on account o' him allus gettin' hurt just when he oughta be at 'is best. Doggone his hide anyway!"

The man laughed lightly.

"Go on! If it wasn't fer me, you'd never have 'ny excitement. Foolin' aside, Marsh, you had any trouble?"

"Oh, no more'n I expected. Th' Wades aren't th' nicest folks in th' world an' they don't like th' idea o' havin' me around.

Reckon that's because they can't savvy my play. 'Course they've made a couple o' tries t' kinda suggest that I hit th' trail...."

"That all?"

"An' they've taken a couple o' pot shots at me," Marshall continued casually. "But, shucks, all in all, they aren't any diff'rent than any o' th' other highbinders I've run up against. They're all hell raisers because everybody gets scared o' th'm an' nobody dares stand up to 'em. They're th' law most o' th' time or they control it, so they get away with pretty much everything."

"Anything you want me t' do?"

Marshall grinned up at him.

"Reckon th' best thing you c'n do right now is take care o' that busted arm o' yourn," he replied. "How many times does this make it?"

"Oh, four or five," Smith answered lightly. "I ain't sure which it is. But it's th' doggonedest thing how I allus manage t' get plugged in my right arm!"

"It's a heap safer gettin' plugged there than any place else," Marshall retorted. "Wouldn't do anybody any good t' try puttin' a bullet through that head o' yourn. It's harder'n rock. I oughta know. Remember th' time I walloped you an' danged near busted my hand on your head?"

"Sure!" Smith said, and he laughed again.

"Ned!" the woman broke in.

"Yeah?"

"Don't you think Smith should send some of his men to help you?" she asked.

"Nuthin' much they could do 'cept mebbe stir up a heap o' suspicions. No, they wouldn't be helpful. Mebbe later on I'll be able t' use 'em, an' if I do need 'em, I'll get word t' Smith an' he can order 'em here."

"Yeah, but don't take any chances an' don't wait till th' last minute t' let me know," Smith said sharply.

Marshall grinned at him.

"Don't worry. I'm awf'lly fond o' life, believe me, an' I don't aim t' have any polecats snuff it out ahead o' time," he retorted. "Besides, th' minute I'm finished here, we're headin' fer California an' nobody's gonna stop us again, not even you, Smith Jenkins!"

"I wish we were on our way again!" the woman said quietly but emotionally.

"We will be," Marshall replied. "An' real soon, too! C'mon, honey; you an' Smith'd better be makin' tracks. You've got a long ways t' go between now an' nightfall."

He took her by the arm, led her back to her horse. The black hovered close by.

"Ned," the woman said, turning to Marshall, "you'll be watchful every minute of the day and night, won't you?"

" 'Course! But I don't want you doin' a heap o' worryin', understand?"

She was in his arms again, clinging to him tightly. His lips brushed her hair.

"It's been so long," she whispered. "It seems like years!"

"I know, honey," he answered. "It's been just as tough on me, believe me, wonderin' what you're doin', what you're thinkin' about an' all that."

Their lips met in a minute-long kiss; then he released her and lifted her into the saddle. He handed her the reins, patted the sorrel's arched neck.

"Take care o' her," he cautioned the sorrel. "Don't forget that!"

He stepped back, and the sorrel wheeled, clattered forward and ranged herself alongside the big white horse. Smith Jenkins settled himself in his saddle, gripping the reins in his left hand.

"So long, Marsh!" he called. "Keep in touch with me an' lemme know right off if you need anything!"

"Goodbye, darling!" the woman called.

The white loped away with the sorrel at his flanks. The black edged forward, rubbed his nose against Marshall's shoulder, but

Marshall gave no sign. He followed the southward racing horses. When they reined in for a moment and both Smith and the woman twisted around in their saddles and waved, he whipped off his hat and waved it vigorously in farewell. Presently, perhaps within a minute's time, they reached the head of the southward trail; when it dipped down sharply, they disappeared from sight. Soon, too, the metallic echo of their horses' hoofs faded out completely. Marshall turned slowly, heavily, and eyed the waiting black, patted the horse's neck.

"Reckon that's that," he said. "We're all alone again."

The big horse pawed the ground.

"Yeah," Marshall said, nodding. "We might's well get goin'. Ain't anything t' keep us here any longer."

He shifted his holsters, reached for the reins and vaulted lightly into the saddle. The black stiffened suddenly and Marshall quickly looked up. A low-pitched whinny broke from the horse; mechanically Marshall's right hand dropped and tightened around the butt of a ready Colt. Now he heard the ring of hoofs on stone and shale and a horse and rider emerged into the clearing from behind a huge boulder. When the rider looked up, Marshall's hand came away from his gun butt; it was Edith Wade. She clattered up and reined in a dozen feet away from him.

"Howdy," he said briefly.

She did not acknowledge his greeting. She shifted herself a bit in her saddle, easing herself. There was a cold, tight-lipped smile on her face. Her eyes ranged over him for a moment.

"The great lover himself," she said coldly, nodding to herself. "I suppose I should apologize for peeping while you were emoting in that so touching farewell scene. Actually, it was quite accidental. You see, I was riding by when you and your lady-love fell into each other's arms, and I simply couldn't go on till the scene was over. I was completely overwhelmed."

He was motionless, and mute, eyeing her quietly and patiently.

"I didn't realize you were such a lady's man," she went on tauntingly, "despite the stories I've heard about you. But now that I've seen you in one of your moments, I know better. Incidentally, that girl was very attractive. And the way she clung to you and kissed you—why, Marshall, I think the silly fool's in love with you! But on the other hand, there's no telling; she may have been playing a rôle, just as you were!"

His eyes glinted dangerously but she disregarded it and went on recklessly.

"She didn't look familiar to me," she continued. "Does she work in one of the saloons in Rainbow? No, I don't think she was one of the local belles. You're far too clever to have her so close to Rainbow. Heavens, think of the complications that might arouse! Suppose Fran Grant were to compare notes with her? That would never do, would it?"

Her horse inched his way closer to the black. Marshall, watching, nudged the black, and the big horse suddenly snorted so frighteningly that Edith's mount, shying away in haste and alarm, almost unseated her. Marshall grinned; he was himself again.

"Wa-al?" he demanded. "You finished? You oughta be, judging by th' way that tongue o' yourns been goin'. Now suppose you just turn aroun' an' go on back where you come from. If you don't, I'm li'ble t' get awful mad. An' when I get mad, th' on'y thing that calms me down is t' give some flannel-mouthed young kid that ain't dry yet behind th' ears a doggoned good spankin'. Go on now—turn that cayuse aroun' an' get outta here."

She bristled, sat upright in the saddle, tightened her grip on the reins. Tiny patches of white anger danced into her flushed cheeks. Suddenly she spurred her horse, which protested, then yielded finally, and bounded forward only to have Marshall swing the black around directly in his path.

"You're goin' th' wrong way," Marshall said curtly. "Turn around."

He leaned forward out of the saddle, grabbed the Wade horse's bridle, and wheeled him.

"There y' are," he said, and released the bridle.

Edith's hand flashed as she slapped Marshall across the face, a stinging, ringing slap. He stared at her wide-eyed; perhaps he was a bit dazed, too. Her horse bolted away like a frightened deer. Edith twisted around in her saddle.

"I hate you!" she screamed. "I hate you!"

He touched his reddened cheek and shook his head.

"Reckon I know how she feels about me," he muttered. He followed her with his eyes. In another minute she was gone, flashing over the range at breakneck speed, racing her mount down a twisting trail that led eastward to the Bar-O. Marshall shook his head again.

"Doggoned hell-cat," he muttered.

He turned slowly, and settled himself in the saddle. The black twisted his head and looked up at him, waiting and wondering. Finally, when Marshall failed to nudge him, the big horse took things upon himself and trotted away. Seeing that Marshall made no attempt to check him, he soon quickened his pace to a brisk canter.

The days that followed passed slowly, long, tedious, uneventful days, and seemingly neverending. Daily, Edith Wade rode the range, hopefully watchful, studying the trails and the blue sky for signs of billowing dust, the wake of a horse's hoofs. From mid-morning until late afternoon she rode slowly through the low country, then up and down trails, but always with the boulder-rimmed clearing as the center of her riding arc. Finally, in the late afternoon, when the chill winds began to sweep down, she would wheel her jaded mount and ride back to the Bar-O.

At home she went about her duties silently. It was natural that Jim and Ed should notice it, and when her back was turned they looked at each other questioningly, and each gave the other the same reply, a shrug of the shoulder.

"What d'you make uv it?" Jim asked one day while Edith was absent from the ranch.

"Dunno what t' make uv it," Ed replied. "I've been noticin' how she hustles outta here right after she gets th' place t' rights, but where'n heck she goes to, I'm doggoned if I c'n even guess."

"Mebbe we oughta ask 'er," Jim suggested hopefully. He hesitated for a moment, then continued, "Ed, reckon I might's well tell you that I followed 'er th' other day. But I'm damned if she did a doggoned thing in th' four hours I trailed 'er but ride up hill an' down, this way an' that, until I was plumb wore out. I was ridin' one o' th' new horses we got, an' th' blamed cayuse ain't himself yet after th' ridin' around I gave 'im. What d'you say we ask 'er, huh?"

Ed shook his head.

"Nope," he said finally, heavily. "We'll just leave 'er alone, leastways fer th' time bein' anyway. Mebbe she's just ridin' somethin' off, somethin' we don't savvy. Y'know, Jim, Pop allus used t' say 'er mother was a loner sometimes, too. He got used to it. When she wanted t' talk, he talked, an' when she acted like she wanted no part uv 'im, he gave 'er a wide berth. Y'know, womenfolks are doggoned mysterious critters. Sometimes they don't even savvy th'mselves, so how'n hell c'n a man do it? Eadie'll get over it an' that'll be that."

"Wa-al, I sure hope so. Say, you don't think she's comin' down with somethin', do you?"

"Huh? Oh, y'mean mebbe she's gettin' somethin'?"

"Could be, couldn't it?" Jim persisted.

"I don't think so," Ed answered. "She's young, an' if I didn't know better, th' on'y thing I'd say was ailin' 'er was that she was in love. But, heck, Jim, you know as well's I do that that's ridiculous. She's just growin' up an' probably don't know what t' make uv it. But give 'er time an' she'll be 'erself again. Just watch an' see if she ain't."

CHAPTER EIGHT
A WOMAN'S CURIOSITY

IT WAS six o'clock in the morning when Marshall, his gun belt in his hand, emerged from the bedroom he shared with Tom Lewis. He buckled the belt around his middle and started toward the kitchen. Since his entry into the Grant household, and since he was an early riser, he had taken it upon himself to prepare the breakfast coffee. Fran generally appeared about seven; fortified with a couple of cups of coffee, Marshall had already found that awaiting her presented no hardship on him. With her appearance on the scene, he retired quite willingly to a nearby chair while she prepared the bacon and eggs or the wheat cakes, or upon occasion, biscuits. He stopped suddenly and sniffed loudly.

"I'll be doggoned!" he muttered in surprise. "Coffee! An' it never smelled better!"

He strode on again, even quickened his stride, and halted a second time, in the kitchen doorway. Fran was busy at the kitchen table, mixing a bowl of batter. It was evidently a "hot cake" morning.

"Hey!" he said in feigned protestation. "What's th' big idea, huh?"

"Of what?" she asked without looking up.

"Of gettin' up so early an' uv hornin' in on my job. I'm supposed t' be th' coffee maker 'round this place, y'know."

"Doesn't it smell good?"

"An' how!" he answered quickly. "But how come?"

"Oh, I just felt that I had had enough sleep, so I got up."

"Wa-al, if that's all, then awright. But don't go makin' a habit uv it. I don't wanna be cut outta my jobs."

"I'll promise to stay in bed till eight tomorrow morning to make up for this morning. All right? And while we're on the subject of getting up early, why do you?"

"Oh, fer no reason 'cept that I've allus been an early riser an' I can't seem t' change my ways."

There was a slow, shuffling step behind him and Tom Lewis appeared, frowned at him, crowded against him in the doorway and peered into the kitchen.

"What'n Sam Hill is goin' on around here?" he demanded. "What's th' idea uv you two gettin' up in th' middle o' th' night, huh?"

Marshall grinned at him.

"Anybody say you hadda get up, too?" he countered.

"Nope, nobody. But how'n blazes is a feller supposed t' sleep when other folks start movin' around an' jawin' away?"

Marshall scoffed loudly.

"Go on! You know danged well you got a whiff o' that coffee an' decided you'd better haul your carcass outta bed an' come get some before it was all gone."

"Could be," Tom answered, and laughed. "Say, Fran, that ain't batter fer hot cakes you're mixin' over there, is it?"

"You know blamed well it is!" Marshall said.

"A feller c'n ask, can't he?"

"Suppose you two sit down," Fran suggested. "The cakes will be ready in a minute."

"Mebbe he don't feel up t' eatin' 'em t'day, Fran?"

"Th' heck I don't!" Tom said quickly. "I c'n eat 'em any time!"

He pushed past Marshall, made his way to the table, swung a chair around and seated himself.

"I'm set," he announced with a grin. "Bring 'em on!"

Marshall sat down.

"Y'know, Tom," he said very seriously, "accordin' t' what I've heard tell, when a feller gets t' be thirty-five he's supposed t' cut down on 'is eatin'. Heck, you're twice that old, so by rights you oughta skip at least one meal a day or mebbe two uv 'em."

"Whoever tol' you that cock an' bull story, Mister, was either plumb loco or just an ornery liar! My ol' man lived t' be more'n eighty an' right up t' his dyin' day he could outeat anybody I ever saw."

"That don't prove a thing! Mebbe if he'da cut down on his eatin' he'd be alive t'day."

"Look, Mister—you afraid there ain't gonna be enough fer a second helpin'?"

"Heck no, Tom! I'm just worryin' about you. I kinda got th' idea when you come in before that you looked sorta drawn an' peaked."

"Doggone it, Fran!" Tom sputtered. "Gimme somethin' t' eat an' pronto, so's I c'n get outta here before this feller talks me into my grave!"

Fran placed stacks of "cakes" in front of each of them and they tackled them with an eager and hungry vengeance.

"Doggone it, Fran!" Tom said after she had given Marshall a second helping. "You don't hafta force 'em on 'im! Wait till he asks fer 'em! After all, a feller c'n on'y eat so much an' after that he's just a glutton if he don't quit!"

"I've another platter full for you, Tom," Fran replied, "whenever you're ready for them."

Old Tom considered for a moment, then shook his head.

"I hate t' turn 'em down," he said finally. "But somehow I don't feel so hungry this mornin'. Give th' rest o' th'm t' Marshall. He don't show it, but he must be all belly judgin' by th' way he packs away grub."

When breakfast was finished, Marshall pushed his chair back from the table and climbed to his feet.

"That was swell, Fran," he said. "You c'n fix hot cakes better'n anybody I know."

He hitched up his pants, shifted his holsters a bit.

"Wa-al, so long fer now," he said, and strode out.

Fran and Tom sat in silence. When they heard the street door open and close behind Marshall, Fran turned quickly to Tom, who, sensing what was coming, averted his eyes.

"Tom!"

"Huh?"

"Tom, where does he go every morning?"

"Who?"

"Marshall," she said very patiently.

"Yuh got me."

"Well, haven't you ever wondered?"

"Nope."

"Oh, Tom!"

"He's free, white an' old enough t' do what he wants to, ain't he?" Tom demanded.

"Yes, of course he is, but doesn't it seem odd to you that he goes off so early every morning?" she persisted.

"Never thought uv it as bein' odd, Fran. I just figger he's got some place t' go an' somethin' t' do when he gets there an' that's all."

"I'm not that easily satisfied. When my curiosity's aroused, I've got to know the whys and the wherefores."

Tom looked up and grinned.

"You wouldn't be a woman if you didn't. But if you're that curious 'bout what he does an' where he goes, why'n thunder don't you ask 'im?"

"You know I can't do that!"

"Uh-huh, so because you're curious I'm supposed t' do th' askin' for yuh—right?"

"Well, it would be more natural for you to ask."

He grinned at her again.

"Don't kid me now. An' don't look at me like that! Y'know danged well it gets me! Doggone it, I allus hafta do th' dirty work! Say, any more coffee left in that pot?"

Fran arose and refilled his cup, then returned to her chair.

"I wish you had asked him this morning," she said after a moment's silence.

"Who? Oh, you still talkin' about Marshall?"

He lowered his eyes quickly, drank his coffee. When he put down the cup again and looked up he found Fran eyeing him.

"Awright," he said. "Awright. I'll ask 'im t'night."

"I still wish you had asked him this morning."

"Doggone it, Fran," he sputtered helplessly, "if it's so important to yuh, why'n heck don't you saddle up an' go after 'im an' see fer yourself where he goes an' what he does? Go on!"

Fran had probably been waiting for him to say just that, for she was out of her chair and out of the room before he realized what he had suggested. He pushed his chair back and got to his feet stiffly.

"Women," he muttered, and shook his head. "I never know what they're gonna do nohow. An' I'm doggoned if they don't do th' doggonedest things!"

A horse clattered past toward the street.

"There she goes, awright," he muttered. "Now I suppose th' thing fer me t' do is t' go after her!"

Topping a rise, Fran had spotted Marshall astride the big black. Quickening her mount's pace, carefully, of course, to avoid being detected, she overtook him, then jerked her horse to a sudden stop when Marshall halted the black. When he dismounted, she did, too. Quickly she led her mount into a thicket, tethered him there, then made her way forward on foot. She crouched down behind some brush that looked down upon the spot where Marshall had dismounted. Now she saw, peering through the twigs, that he had seated himself on a rock.

"He's waiting for someone," she decided shortly. Then the disturbing and frightening thought came to her that he was waiting for a woman.

The ground sloped away from where Marshall idled on a gentle incline. At the bottom of the incline there were tall trees; from where she crouched, Fran could see the tops of them. Marshall got to his feet, hitched up his belt, and started down the incline. The black looked up, swung over behind him, and followed at his heels. Fran was undecided now. Should she follow, too, or should she stifle her curiosity and go home? Perhaps she shouldn't have come in the first place. But since she had, perhaps she would be better off not knowing whom he was awaiting. But she admitted that wouldn't do at all. The knowledge that he was to meet someone there would madden her unless she knew who the woman was. She followed him with her eyes until presently he disappeared from sight. Suddenly she heard the echo of an approaching horse's hoofs and crouched down even lower than before. The metallic clatter swelled and finally, when she could restrain herself no longer, she raised her head. A horse and rider appeared, and her eyes widened.

"Eadie!" she gasped. "Eadie Wade! He's been meeting her every morning!"

For a moment she was speechless. The enormity of her discovery overwhelmed her and left her briefly weak and crushed. The thought that she might be jealous never occurred to her. She knew only that she was hurt and angry, but she made no attempt to analyze her feelings beyond that point. The fact that he had come there to meet another woman was the all-important thing, and it made her furious. Marshall, because he hadn't told anyone—she meant herself, of course—of his secret rendezvous with Edith Wade, had betrayed her. Not that Edith Wade mattered. It could have been another woman—even one she didn't know—and she would have felt just as angry. It was in short, she told herself, just the principle of the thing, and she was bitter.

Now she followed Edith with her angry eyes, saw her ride past the rock on which Marshall had sat but minutes before, saw her ride slowly down the incline. Fran's lip curled scornfully.

"They've certainly arranged their meetings beautifully," she said half aloud. "He gets here ahead of her, waits a few minutes, then rides down into the trees. She appears as arranged, looking as innocent as a baby, and follows him down to their hidden meeting place. Oh, it's so cheap, it simply sickens me!"

She straightened up, wheeled and started away. She did not look back. Edith had almost neared the trees when she heard a step on some loose shale and whirled around in the saddle. She caught a fleeting glimpse of Fran Grant, saw her head for a nearby thicket and disappear within it. As she watched, Fran reappeared astride her horse, spurred him and set him dashing away. Edith's eyes widened.

"I wonder what she was doing out here?" she asked herself.

Fran disappeared in the distance and Edith finally settled herself in the saddle. Slowly she went on. It was so still among the trees. She jerked her horse to an abrupt stop when she heard another horse whinny. It startled her and she looked about her quickly. There was a movement close by and a big black horse appeared. She recognized him at once, realized it was Marshall's horse. Her eyes blazed. Now she knew what Fran Grant had been doing out there.

"Meeting out here in secret!" she said angrily.

She wheeled her horse, dug her heels into his flanks, and sent him racing up the incline. When he slackened his pace, she vented her anger upon him, lashing him with the loose ends of the reins.

"Of all the low, contemptible things!" she said aloud. "The righteous Miss Grant!"

It was Fran, the thought of her, that infuriated her. She lashed her horse again, and he thundered past the rock on which Marshall had sat, burst through the brush; then, when Edith jerked the reins, he raced away eastward. For a lingering moment the swift clatter of his hoofs echoed over the range; then it faded gently, and presently died out completely. But now a horseman, old Tom Lewis, appeared some fifty feet away. He clattered forward, twisted around in the saddle and, satisfied that he was alone, relaxed again. He pulled up almost at the very spot where Fran had crouched, and looked about him. There was no sign of Marshall. There was a faint smile on his face. Presently he laughed softly, shook his head.

"That was just about th' doggonedest funniest thing I ever seen," he muttered, and laughed again. "First Fran come ridin' outta here hell bent fer election, then Eadie Wade."

He nudged his horse with his knees, and they broke through the brush and started down the incline. Tom grinned again.

"Wonder what happened? Wouldn't do t' ask Fran when I see 'er. Better pretend I don't know from nuthin'. That'll help keep th' peace. Still, I wish Marshall was aroun'. Bet he could tell me what all that there fast ridin' was about."

He laughed, slowed his horse a bit.

"Th' way I figger it, both Fran an' Eadie musta come out here fer th' same purpose. It makes sense t' me, 'cause I know from th' look in Fran's eye that she's after Marshall. As fer Eadie, 'course she's on'y a youngster, but that Marshall feller's got a way with 'im an' mebbe Eadie's fallen fer 'im, too. No tellin' with women."

He pushed his hat back from his eyes. When they came to the trees at the foot of the incline he halted his mount. He looked about him for a moment, relaxed in the saddle. His thoughts went back over the years and the memory of those days brought a smile to his face.

"This here bus'ness makes me think o' Jim Patrick's girls," he mused. "Heck, that must be more'n forty years ago if it was a day. Jim had three girls. There was Annie, Lizzie an' Jennie. They were all 'bout seventeen; that is, Annie an' Jennie were seventeen, twins at that. Seems t' me Lizzie was about a year older.

Anyway, th' three o' th'm kinda fell fer th' same feller. Doggone it—what'n heck was his name? Lawson, I think, or mebbe it was Dawson. What I do remember is that Jim had one helluva time with them kids o' his. They coulda cut each other's throats. There was a helluva lot o' slappin' an' scratchin' an' hair pullin' an' they plumb near got Jim loco. Then right in th' middle o' everything, this Lawson or Dawson feller ups an' gets 'imself hitched t' some widow woman an' that was th' end o' that. Sure was funny while it lasted. On'y one who couldn't see it thataway was Jim, poor feller. I know I got a heck uva kick out uv it, but I don't suppose I'da done any laughin' if them kids were mine."

Tom nudged his horse. They swerved away from the trees, coming to an abrupt stop when the black suddenly appeared.

"Oh, yeah?" Tom muttered, eyeing the big horse. "So Marshall is aroun' here after all, eh? Mebbe we'd better climb down an' kinda mosey aroun' a bit an' see what this is all about?"

He swung himself out of the saddle. The black, watching him, backed away slowly, and finally turned and trotted off. Tom, quickening his pace, followed. The big horse stopped and looked back; when he saw that Tom was coming toward him, he threw up his head and whinnied, then wheeled and dashed away.

"Hol' on, doggone yuh!" Tom panted.

Following in the black's steps, Tom came upon a wall of brush. He stopped short, breathing heavily, and made his way around the brush until he came to a breakthrough. Twenty feet off shore was a swift stream. Tom's eyes widened. In the very middle of the stream, a naked body, a lean, tanned body, cut through the water, then turned over. As Tom watched, Marshall passed on his back. A laugh arose in Tom's throat but he choked it off hastily by clapping his hand over his mouth. He backed off, wheeled and strode swiftly away.

"There y'are," he muttered, and shook his head. "That shows yuh what an innocent thing like takin' a swim c'n lead to. Just because he hightails it outta th' house so early every mornin', Fran's probably got it figgered out that he comes all th' way up here fer 'nother purpose. An' now that she an' Eadie bumped into each other up here, I'll bet each one thinks Marshall's meetin' th' other up here an' romancin' 'er! Doggone women anyway!"

CHAPTER NINE

MARSHALL GETS DOWN TO CASES

Mike Gallo was standing in the open doorway of the Star when Marshall emerged from the bank and came sauntering up the street.

"Mornin'," Gallo said briefly. Marshall nodded to him in reply. "How's things?"

Marshall halted, hooked his thumbs in his belt.

"Oh, awright," he answered. "Hear o' anybody else bein' on th' prowl fer me since th' sheriff tried t' pin that Bendix killin' on me as a murder?"

Gallo grinned. His white, even teeth flashed brightly when his lips parted.

"Nope. Reckon you've been behavin' yourself, eh?"

"I usu'lly do."

" 'Course," he said quickly. "Say, Marshall, you plannin' t' stay on in Rainbow?"

"Dunno. Haven't made up my mind yet. Why?"

"Wa-al, you don't look t' me like the kind o' feller who c'n be satisfied just hangin' aroun' an' doin' nuthin'."

"Thanks," Marshall said dryly.

"I ain't finished yet. Jim Lane who owns th' X-Bar-X spread was in here last night an' told me his foreman's quittin'. Lane's a pretty square shooter an' the job's worth c'nsidering if you ain't plannin' t' hightail it. Th' pay's good an' its allus on th' line when payday comes around. That's more'n I c'n say 'bout most bosses I've heard tell of."

Marshall nodded in agreement.

"I wouldn't mind puttin' in a good word for you, Marshall, an' it might mean somethin' with Lane. We've been good friends fer a long time. But before I say anything t' Lane, I'd like t' know that if you take th' job it wouldn't be just fer a spell, say t' tide you over till you got some foldin' money in your kick, an' that then you'd hit th' trail. I wouldn't wanna do that t' Lane because he wants a feller permanent. What d'you think?"

"How soon does he hafta know?"

"Oh, in a couple o' days."

"Then suppose I think about it an' let you know?"

"Swell. He'll be in town again 'bout th' end o' th' week. You lemme know before that."

"I'll do that, an' thanks fer thinkin' o' me fer th' job."

"Forget it," Gallo said with a dismissing gesture of his hand. "Wa-al, reckon I'd better get things org'nized inside. Stop by again an' lemme know what t' do about that job."

"Wait a minute," Marshall said quickly. "If you got another minute t' spare, I'd like t' ask you somethin', Gallo. You mind?"

"Nope," the cafe owner answered. "Go 'head. What's botherin' you?"

"It's about Fran Grant's father an' th' bank."

"Oh! Look, Marshall, suppose we go inside? It's a heap easier t' talk in there."

"Whatever you say."

Gallo turned and led the way into the cafe; Marshall followed at his heels. They halted at the bar and leaned over it.

"How 'bout a drink?" Gallo asked. "My own stuff, y'know."

Marshall shook his head.

"Too early in th' day fer me," he replied. "Gallo, I wanna know what you know about Grant an' th' bank."

"Don't know much, Marshall. I had some dough in there same's most everybody else in town did. When th' place was robbed, that was th' end o' my dough an' of th' others'. But that's all I c'n tell you."

"Th' Wades've been yelpin' fer all they're worth that it was Grant 'imself who robbed th' bank an' that Fran was either in on it or knows where 'er pop cached th' dough. What's your opinion?"

"Haven't got any."

"Come on, Gallo—don't gimme that."

The big man shrugged his shoulders.

"You asked me an' I answered you th' on'y way I know," he said doggedly. "What d'you want me t' do? Want me t' tell you what somebody else says or what I think about it?"

"I don't give a damn fer what anybody else says. I wanna know what you know," Marshall retorted.

"Awright then. You just remember that I got th' Star t' watch over so's it don't just move out on me. That, Mister, is a full-time job, believe me, an' handlin' that don't leave me time fer mindin' anybody else's bus'ness. How'n hell would I know what Grant was doin' over t' his place or what he was cookin' up? He never came in here. An' th' on'y time I ever saw him was when I went over t' th' bank t' deposit some dough an' that wasn't often."

"Yeah, but—"

" 'Course I've heard a lotta talk since th' robbery, but what uv it? Th' Wades c'n holler all they wanna, but it don't prove anything, does it?"

"Gallo, d'you think it was an outside job?"

"It could've been. An' it could've been any one uv mebbe a dozen hombres right here in Rainbow who could've done th' job. But that don't prove anything either, does it?"

"Quit stallin'. You hear a lot o' them shootin' off their mouths when they're drunk, so you oughta know somethin'."

Gallo eyed him for a moment.

"What's your angle, Marshall?" he asked presently. "What are you after?"

"Haven't got any angles an' I don't figger t' get a damned thing out uv it."

"I'm still listenin'."

"You c'n believe this or not, but all I'm tryin' t' do is help Fran Grant out uv a lousy mess."

"You're a stranger here, Marshall. Why are you buttin' into somethin' that don't concern you?"

"I'm buttin' into it because th' hull thing smells bad t' me an' because it all centers aroun' a girl who can't fight back. Want any more reasons?"

Gallo seemed to be smiling.

"Who d'you think robbed th' bank, Marshall?" he asked.

"Who?" Marshall echoed loudly. "Th' Wades, that's who! They killed Grant, robbed th' bank, an' now they're hollerin' bloody murder just t' cover th'mselves up. Th' hull thing's so dog-goned crooked, it—it stinks out loud!"

"An' supposin' they did everything you say they did, Marshall," Gallo went on quietly. "What c'n you do about it?"

"Dunno yet, but mebbe I c'n cook up somethin'."

Gallo was silent for a moment, eyeing Marshall thoughtfully, appraisingly. Presently he nodded.

"Uh-huh," he said. "Mebbe you can."

"I will!"

Gallo's thick fingers drummed on the surface of the bar.

"Marshall," he said finally, "I believe you. I think you're on th' level."

"You know damn' well I am," Marshall said evenly.

"An' because I think you're on th' level," Gallo continued, "I'm gonna give you a lead."

"Now you're talkin'!"

"You understan', uv course, that if anybody ever gets wind o' this, that'll be th' end o' me?"

Marshall stiffened.

"Nobody's ever accused me o' talkin' outta turn," he said sharply. "Or o' talkin' too much."

"That's what I'm bankin' on," Gallo went on calmly. "An' that's why I'm gonna back your play. 'Course I'll hafta keep in th' background, but you'll understan' that I'm on'y doin' that t' stay alive. We better have that understood right off."

"Awright—that's settled."

Gallo looked toward the door; then he bent closer to Marshall.

"Jim Wade," he whispered.

"Huh? What d'you mean—Jim Wade?"

"Sh-h-h!" Gallo cautioned him. "You don't hafta holler, y'know!"

Marshall gave him a cold stare.

"Awright!" he said gruffly, then in a lower tone of voice: "Now what was that about Jim Wade?"

"He's th' man fer you t' work on."

"Y'mean he did th' job?"

"Nope. I dunno just what he did 'cept that he did somethin'."

"Yeah, but—"

"Look, Marshall, I know what I'm doin', so just take things th' way I give 'em to you; then we'll get somewheres. I didn't hafta t' be a witness to it t' know that th' Wades engineered th' robbin' an' th' killin'. I just know they did it an' let it go at that."

"Awright, Gallo—let's get back t' Jim Wade."

"I said 'Jim Wade' because I know from experience that he's th' easier one o' th' two brothers t' handle. Put th' pressure on 'im, scare th' pants o' 'im, an' he'll spill his guts out. Get th' idea?"

"Yeah," Marshall said slowly, thoughtfully. "Sure."

"I dunno how or when you're gonna get t' him," Gallo continued. "But you'll hafta work that out fer yourself."

"Jim Wade," Marshall mused.

"He's your man."

Marshall hitched up his pants. Gallo watched him, watched him shift his twin holsters a bit.

"Wa-al," Marshall said finally with a quiet grin, "now I've got somethin' to work on."

Gallo shrugged.

"It's a starter," he admitted. "But how far you get with what y'know depends on how smart y'are. Just you remember that th' Wades are ornery an' that they've got a lot o' friends 'round these parts. You're a loner, an' you're gonna find that everybody's against you. If you get away with what you're gonna hafta do, an' with a hull skin, you'll be luckier'n all hell. Wa-al, so long, Marshall, an' good luck. 'Less I miss my guess, you're gonna need a heap uv it!"

Gallo pulled his horse to an abrupt stop. He had heard approaching hoof beats; now he could see the hatted head and the shoulders of a horseman coming toward him, swinging through a rocky pass. He stood up in his stirrups and looked eagerly.

"Jim!" he yelled, and dropped down into his saddle.

He dug his spurs into his horse's flanks, sent him bounding forward. The oncoming man rode into the open; it was Jim Wade. He looked up, recognized Gallo and waved in answer to the cafe owner's yell of recognition. Presently Gallo came dashing up.

"H'llo, Mike," Jim called, and pulled up. He seemed surprised to see Gallo and added: "What are you doin' out this way? Didn't know you ever went sight-seein' or callin'."

Gallo halted his mount, wheeled him around and ranged him alongside Wade's.

"I come out here just t' see you, Jim," he replied. "I was hopin' I'd run into you away from th' ranch."

Wade's eyebrows arched.

"Yeah? Why?"

Gallo eased himself in the saddle and shoved his hat back from his eyes. Jim did likewise, almost mechanically.

"Got somethin' I wanted t' talk t' you about. Somethin' personal an' private."

"Oh," Jim said, and waited.

"It's about Marshall."

Jim's face clouded.

"Marshall?" he repeated. "What about 'im, th' skunk?"

"We'll come t' him in a minute, Jim," Gallo said. "First there's somethin' else. You an' me've been friends fer a long time, ain't we?"

"Yeah, sure."

"Must be more'n ten years."

"More or less, but what's that gotta do with Marshall?" Jim demanded. "I don't savvy th' connection."

Gallo smiled patiently.

"You will in a minute, Jim," he continued. "I just wanted t' remind you o' how long we've been friends because what I gotta say t' you, I want you t' take th' way one friend'd take from another. That awright?"

"Reckon so—leastways, it is so far."

"Then let's go on. Jim, you've allus had t' play second fiddle t' Ed. That's right, ain't it?"

Jim Wade frowned. He eyed Gallo sharply now.

"Go on," he said curtly.

"Not that I don't think a heap o' Ed," Gallo went on reassuringly. "I do, believe me, because they don't come 'ny better'n Ed. It's just that I like both o' you an' somethin' come up an' I think you oughta be th' man t' do it an' grab off some o' th' thunder fer yourself fer a change."

"I'm still listenin'," Jim said.

"Jim, th' feller who gets Marshall'll be just about th' biggest thing in this county. 'Course if that perticular feller should be either you or Ed that'll be natural. If it happens t' be somebody else, he'll be bigger'n you an' Ed by a mile. That right?"

"Yeah," Jim admitted. "I s'ppose so."

Gallo smiled; then he braced himself.

"Jim, you could be that feller easy," he said quietly. "You're better'n most with a six-gun, heaps better'n Ed if it ever came to a test. You just ain't never had t' step out on your own an' show folks just what you could do if you had to."

Wade looked at him and grinned.

"Hey, Mike—are you tryin' t' kid me?" he demanded.

"Nope," Gallo answered. "I've been hearin' a lot o' other folks sayin' doggoned nice things about you, Jim, an' it kinda got me t' thinkin'. An' th' more I thought about th' idea, th' more I become convinced that you're just th' feller t' take Marshall an' get Rainbow back t' normal."

Jim did not answer. He looked away quietly, tight-lipped and thoughtful.

"Marshall ain't half as good as folks like t' make him out," Gallo went on shortly. "An', Jim, in this case, it wouldn't have t' be an even draw. Savvy?"

Jim turned to him again quickly.

"Y'mean—"

"You could get th' drop on 'im an' then pour it into 'im."

"Yeah, I suppose so."

"He comes into th' Star regular," Gallo continued. "Now if you were t' drop in, say, in th' evenin', pay no attention to 'im, kinda make your way up t' th' bar so's he wouldn't get suspicious, jerk out your gun an' give it to 'im, that'd be that, an' you'd be top man. What do you say, Jim?"

"Ed know anything o' this?"

"Nope," Gallo answered. "I ain't seen Ed fer some time now. What's more, I don't want to till this thing's over. Jim, just picture it fer yourself—walkin' into th' ranchhouse an' sayin' t' Ed, 'Wa-al, that's that. I just got Marshall.' C'n you picture Ed, hearin' that? Heck!"

There was a cold, hard smile on Jim's face. Unconsciously his hand dropped and tightened around the butt of his gun, tightened around it so viciously that it seemed crushed in his huge hand.

"Yeah, Mike," he said presently, almost breathlessly. "I think Mister Marshall's about t' get what's due 'im. An' I'm gonna be th' feller t' give it to 'im!"

Gallo laughed softly and clapped Jim on his broad back.

"Good fer you!" he said heartily. "Let's shake on it!"

They gripped hands for a moment. Then Gallo straightened up in his saddle.

"T'morrow night'd be a good time, Jim," he said. "I'll see to it that Marshall's there. An', Jim—"

"Yeah?"

"I'd make sure if I was you that Ed didn't know anything 'bout this so's he couldn't bust in ahead o' you an' spoil things. Y'know, Ed's allus kinda jealous o' anybody gettin' ahead o' him, an' you know what he'd do t' be th' one t' kill Marshall. He'd give everything he's got fer th' honor o' bein' known as th' feller who killed Marshall."

"I know," Jim said quickly, responsively. "I know, on'y this time Ed's gonna have t' take my smoke. This is gonna be my party, all mine!"

"An' I'll have somethin' on hand t' help make that party th' doggonedest biggest party Rainbow's ever had! Be seein' you, Jim!"

CHAPTER TEN
STORM CLOUDS

IT WAS late afternoon. Edith had returned from her daily ride, and now, her horse unsaddled and turned loose in the corral, she was standing at the fence behind the barn, staring moodily into space. She looked skyward listlessly. Soon it would be evening. Lengthening shadows had already made their appearance; she could see them draping their veils over the range, over the house beyond the corral. She was tired and the thought of preparing supper sickened her. But she forced herself to turn around, started slowly toward the house. She passed the barn, stopping when she heard a voice within. Curiosity forced her to walk to the open doorway, to peer inside. For a moment she could distinguish nothing in the barn's shadowy dimness. The voice gritted again presently, and it guided her eyes to the last stall at the far end of the barn. It was Jim's voice, and now she could see him, a huge, hulking figure of a man. He was just outside the stall, facing it, crouching strangely like a great shaggy lion about to spring. He moved suddenly, cat-like despite his bulk, and she saw a leveled gun flash into his right hand. Her eyes widened.

"Yeah, Marshall," she heard Jim say curtly. "It's me, Jim Wade. You musta figgered it'd be you an' me some day. Reckon this is th' day, awright, an' it means th' end o' th' trail fer you. 'Course, if you wanna, go right ahead an' reach fer them Colts o' yourn. I'm gonna kill you anyway, but it'll look a heap better fer me if you make some kind o' play, y'know."

Edith was over the threshold now.

Jim laughed softly.

" 'Smatter?" he taunted. "Fraid t' move, eh? Wa-al, mebbe it's just as well. You other fellers—g'wan, get outta there an' over t' th' other side o' th' room. I'm gonna start blastin' in a minute an' I don't wanna splatter this skunk's guts all over you."

He laughed again, then stopped abruptly and whirled around when he heard Edith's quick step on the creaking floor boards.

"Oh," he said quickly, sheepishly. "Didn't hear you come in, Eadie."

She swept past him now, peered into the stall, then turned and looked at him.

"Oh, Jim!" she said, almost reproachfully.

He flushed beneath her steady eyes. She leaned back against the wall. He looked away, holstered his gun awkwardly, hitchd up his pants, then jerked his head up and faced her again defintly, doggedly.

"Go ahead an' laugh if you wanna," he said gruffly. "It's awright. I won't get mad. But mebbe t'morrow it'll be diff'rent. Mebbe then I'll do all th' laughin' 'round here."

"What—what do you mean?"

"Nuthin'," he said quickly; then a shrewd gleam brightened his eyes. He laughed softly.

"Nuthin' a-tall."

She eyed him for another moment; then she stepped past him, marched to the door, reached the doorway and stopped. Jim, at her heels, crowded against her.

"Ed," she said simply.

He peered over her shoulder and saw his brother trudging up the path toward the house. For a moment Jim watched him, tight-lipped and silent; then Ed reached the house and went in.

"Eadie," he said.

"Yes?" she asked over her shoulder.

"You go on up t' th' house, too. It's most suppertime anyway. If Ed asks fer me, you just say you ain't seen me. Say it like you mean it, understand?"

She turned to him.

"But aren't you coming in for—?"

He shook his head.

"No," he answered. "I'll skip supper fer t'night. If I'm hungry, I c'n eat later on. Right now I gotta get goin'. Got somethin' to 'tend to."

"You're going to Rainbow?"

"Yeah," he said grimly. "I'm gonna take care o' Mister Marshall t'night. But I don't want a peep outta you about it, y'hear, t' Ed or anybody else."

She stared at him, and he mistook the expression in her widened eyes and on her face for worry about him.

"It's awright," he said quickly, reassuringly. "Nuthin's gonna happen t' me. Everything's arranged. Just remember what I told you an' I'll see you later."

He patted her shoulder clumsily, then pushed past her out of the barn and tramped away toward the corral. His horse, already saddled, was tied up just inside the corral gate. Edith saw him climb into the saddle, wheel and ride out of the corral. He spurred his horse, rode westward at a gallop. Presently he was out of sight.

A sob burst from Edith. She plunged out of the barn, raced blindly toward the corral. She flung open the gate. There were a dozen horses idling close by and they looked up, shied and backed away. Her own horse turned his head and looked at her; he alone did not move. Her saddle lay against a nearby post and she snatched it up, swung it over her horse's back. A minute later, astride her mount, she came whirling out of the corral, spurred the horse and sent him racing away after Jim. Two men came out of the bunkhouse, stopped and looked up, following her swift flight with puzzled eyes.

"H'm," one man muttered. "Looks like she's in one helluva sweat t' get somewheres, don't it?"

"Uh-huh," his companion answered.

"An' she's ruinin' some mighty good horse-flesh gettin' there," the first man continued. "Y'know, Buck, I've been watchin' that young un th' last couple o' days, an' if anybody was t' ask me, she's—"

"Who's askin' you?" the second man said gruffly.

"Nobody, but—"

"Then why don't you ferget it?"

"Fer Pete's sake, what is this? Th' first time I open my mouth; I get stepped on."

"That's a heap easier on you than havin' somethin' else happen to you. Long's you work fer th' Wades, don't go shootin' off your mouth 'bout any o' th'm."

"But I wasn't doin' no such thing!"

"Mebbe not, Danny, but I wasn't takin' any chances. You don't know th' Wades like I do. From now on, take my advice, partner—don't go passin' no opinions 'bout anything 'round here. You just remember that an' you'll live longer an' happier. Savvy? Awright then—come on."

Edith rode swiftly onward. Mile after mile fell away behind her; then suddenly she swerved her horse and sent him racing away in a southerly direction. After a mile she swung westward again. She twisted around in the saddle and looked back. Her heart beat faster, happily, for there was no sign of Jim. Her southward, circling ride had brought her safely past him, and now, if she could maintain her pace, she would reach Rainbow ahead of him. It was dusk now and the thought of the approaching, deepening darkness frightened her. She leaned forward and patted her horse's neck. He seemd to understand, seemed too to quicken his pace in answer to her touch. Suddenly she realized that it was cooler, and she wished she had had time to slip on her jacket. A vagrant leaf, caught up by a sudden breeze, spun by within inches of her horse's head; frightened, he jerked away. He stumbled awkwardly, momentarily, and she screamed and clutched the saddle horn frantically with both hands; but fortunately, her mount kept his feet. When the moment had passed safely, she relaxed once more, bowed and spent.

They thundered over a grassless stretch of ground and the racing horse's hoofs echoed metallically over the darkening range. Then, just as suddenly, they were sweeping onward through thick, lush grass again and his flashing hoofs were muffled. She felt stronger now and she raised her head. In the distance, a little below them, she could see a glow of dimmed yellowish lights. It was Rainbow. In a few minutes they were going down a gentle, grassy slope; minutes later they were racing up the street toward the bank.

There were men on both sides of the street, lounging, idling, talking men; there were men standing in lighted doorways . . . they looked up when she dashed past them, turned and watched her interestedly. They saw her pull up in front of the bank, saw her slip to the ground and scamper across the sidewalk to the bank's door. They saw her fling it open and burst in. They looked at one another. There was no voiced comment, no reaction save a simple shrugging of shoulders, and in some few instances, an equally expressive arching of eyebrows.

"Edith!" Fran said in surprise from the connecting doorway between the bank proper and the living quarters beyond it. "This is a surprise!"

Edith whirled and stared at her.

"Where is he?" she demanded breathlessly.

"He?" Fran repeated.

"Marshall!" Edith said impatiently.

"Oh!"

"Fran, I must see him at once! It's important—terribly important!"

"Really!"

Their eyes met and clashed. There was excitement, emotion, even rising anger in Edith's eyes; Fran's were steadier, calmer and more restrained.

"I'm sorry," Fran said finally, "but he isn't here at the moment. However, I'll be glad to give him a message if you care to leave one."

There was a brief, second-long silence.

"Do you know where he is?" Edith pressed eagerly. "Or where he's gone?"

Fran smiled coldly.

"No," she replied, "I don't. Actually, I don't consider his going and coming any of my business. He isn't married to me, you know. He's merely an employee of the bank."

Edith's lip curled scornfully. At the words "employee of the bank," she turned her head and looked about her. The vast emptiness of the "bank" and its complete lack of everything save a single low counter brought a fleeting smile to her face. Fran disregarded it completely. She waited patiently, unhurried and unruffled, until Edith faced her again.

"And now," she continued, "I hope you will excuse me. Of course, I shall tell Marshall that you were here. Doubtless he'll be sorry he missed you."

Edith turned slowly. Fran smiled again, watched the younger girl for another moment.

"Perhaps you'd like to wait for him?" she asked. "Of course, I must warn you that it may be a matter of hours, perhaps even days; however—"

Edith looked at her over her shoulder.

"Jim," she said quietly and simply, "is on his way here to kill him."

There was no reply from Fran, no visible reaction, no outward movement. Suddenly she smiled again; then she laughed softly.

"Really?" she said, and laughed again. "That's the most amusing thing I've ever heard. Here you are, a Wade, someone who tried to kill him once, expecting me to believe such a childish story. Do you think I'm as naïve as all that, to believe such a story from you and about your own brother? Really, Edith, that's asking too much of me! Frankly, I'm glad, for your sake, of course, that Marshall isn't here. I know what his reaction would be and I'm glad you're saved the embarrassment of hearing it. Must you be going?"

Edith, her face flushed with anger, wheeled and marched to the door. But in the doorway she halted again for a final word.

"You may tell him—" she began icily.

"Yes, my dear?" Fran called tauntingly. "I may tell him what?"

Edith's jaws snapped shut. She stormed out, returned almost immediately and pulled the door shut. She dashed across the sidewalk and swung up into the saddle, wheeled her mount, spurred him and sent him racing up the street. Men turned and looked at her, but she saw none of them. It was only when she thundered past the Star that she pulled up abruptly. Jim's horse was tied up at the rail. For a moment she stared at the horse; then she settled back in the saddle and dashed out of town.

In the bank Fran Grant was standing stiffly, motionlessly, still facing the closed door. She whirled suddenly.

"Tom!" she screamed. "Tom!"

The old man appeared in the connecting doorway.

"Yeah, Fran?"

She ran to him, grasped his arms.

"Tom," she gasped. "You must find Marshall. You must, you understand? Jim Wade is on his way here to kill him!"

CHAPTER ELEVEN

PLOT AND COUNTERPLOT

JIM WADE, his face flushed, leaned over the bar. He caught up the bottle in front of him and poured himself another drink. Mike Gallo was standing at the far end of the bar, his eyes fixed on the open doorway. The bartender nudged him and Mike looked at him questioningly, then followed the bartender's eyes toward the bottle in front of Jim.

"Give 'im another one?" The bartender's lips framed the words without actually voicing them.

Gallo nodded, and the bartender whisked a bottle off the shelf behind him, uncorked it and placed it on the bar. Jim drained his glass.

"That fer me?" he asked, eyeing the second bottle interestedly.

"Yep," the bartender replied. He removed the empty bottle, filled Jim's glass with whiskey from the second bottle. "There y'are, partner. Drink 'er down!"

Jim grinned broadly. His beady eyes seemed to gleam all the brighter in his liquor-flushed face.

"Leave that t' me!" he said. He lifted the glass. "Here's mud in your eye!"

He swallowed the drink and put down the glass. Mike Gallo sidled up to him, nudged him.

"Jim!"

"Yeah?"

"He's back," Gallo whispered.

"Huh? Oh, y'mean Marshall?"

"Yep. He just rode past. He's probably reached th' bank by now."

"Uh-huh."

"Wa-al?" Gallo pressed him.

"What d'you figger I oughta do? Go after 'im?"

"What d'you figger you oughta do?"

Jim straightened up, hitched up his belt, shifted his holster a bit.

"Wa-al, reckon this is it," he said grimly.

Gallo clapped him on the back.

"An' you'll do it, too!" he said. "My dough's on you, Jim. I ain't never picked th' wrong man yet an' I don't aim t' spoil that record now. Go ahead an' get it over with!"

Jim nodded. He turned slowly and started toward the door; midway he quickened his pace and strode out. Gallo smiled fleetingly. The bartender reached for the bottle, checked himslf, looked at Gallo.

"Want a drink, Boss?" he asked.

Gallo turned his head.

"Huh? A drink?" he repeated. "Yeah, Charley, I'll have a drink. I think I got one comin' to me!"

The bartender eyed him curiously, and wisely refrained from saying anything. He produced a clean glass, filled it and shoved it across the bar.

"There y'are, Boss," he said.

Gallo nodded and lifted the glass to his lips.

"Here's how!"

"How!" Charley said.

Gallo swallowed the drink, reached for the bottle and refilled his glass.

Marshall dismounted, led the black down the alley that ran alongside the bank, then around the building to the lean-to behind it. Tom Lewis appeared in the doorway of the lean-to.

"I've been lookin' all over fer you," he said directly. "You seen anything o' Jim Wade?"

"Nope."

"Seen anything o' Eadie Wade?"

Marshall shook his head.

"Jim's in town," Tom continued. "Better watch yourself. He's here t' get you."

"Ed with 'im?"

"Nope. Jim's playin' this string out all by 'imself."

"An' Eadie?"

"She come into town ahead o' Jim. She come straight t' th' bank t' warn you 'bout Jim."

The expression on Marshall's face reflected his surprise.

"Eadie did?"

Old Tom grinned.

"Uh-huh. She an' Fran opened up on each other, an' fer a minute I kinda expected I'd hafta dig me a hole somewheres t' crawl into t' keep from bein' scalped. I was inside, but I didn't let on I could hear th'm. Say, Marshall, mebbe you don't know it, an' if you do, mebbe you don't care a hoot, but both o' them girls are in love with you."

"Now it's two o' th'm, eh?"

"Uh-huh. I tol' you before, I c'n read th' signs. This time I didn't hafta read anything. I heard 'em an' right out loud, too, an' there was no mistakin' 'em. Fran's jealous as a cat an' she sure showed it. 'Course I was kinda surprised t' hear Eadie talk up. I had her pegged as bein' just a mite too young fer that sort o' thing, but now that I think uv it—hell, no female's too young or too old fer romancin'!"

Tom patted the black's neck.

"What'n hell d'you do t' women t' make 'em act up like that, huh?" he demanded. "I'm doggoned if I c'n figger it out. From what I've seen an' heard, you don't seem t' lead 'em on or encourage 'em any, but I'm damned if they still don't fall

all over th'mselves declarin' th'mselves in on you. I'm plumb stumped!"

Marshall laughed lightly, and unsaddled the black.

"Y'know," Tom continued, "when I was a young feller, I used t' think I was a top hand with th' women. But, heck, you got me beat a dozen diff'rent ways from th' ace when it comes t' breakin' hearts. Th' on'y way I c'n figger it out is that it's shyin' away from women th' way you do that gets 'em. It must be!"

Marshall stepped to the doorway of the lean-to and dropped the saddle just inside the door.

"I used t' think women liked big, rough he-men," Tom went on. " 'Sweep 'em off their feet,' was th' way I went after 'em. But now I c'n see that that was all wrong. Your way's a heap better. Wa'al, you live an' you learn, eh, Marshall?"

"Where's Jim Wade now?" the latter asked.

"Huh? Jim? Oh, he's down t' th' Star sloppin' up that rat poison Mike Gallo sells fer whiskey. I poked my head in there when I come past a little while ago, an' from what I could see uv 'im, Jim was doin' awright fer 'imself."

Marshall had listened attentively; now he nodded.

"If that's th' way it is," he remarked, "then th' chances are he won't be lookin' fer anything but a place t' sleep it off."

"Dunno about that," Tom said quickly, warningly. "What's more, I wouldn't even count on it neither. There's no tellin' with them Wades. Th' on'y thing you c'n figger on far's they're concerned is that they're mean an' ornery an' that if you give th'm a break, you're a sucker."

"I don't aim t' give th'm anything," Marshall said determinedly. "Leastways, no more'n I have to. I know their kind. You either kill them or you get killed. It's that simple."

Tom nodded in agreement.

"That's right. So if Jim shows up here an' he makes just one move, give it to 'im good an' proper. Th' sooner th' Wades get killed off, th' sooner Rainbow c'n settle down t' livin'."

There was a sudden shout from the direction of the street; the two looked at each other.

"What d'you s'ppose that is?" Marshall asked.

Old Tom snorted.

"You oughta know th' answer t' that one," he retorted.

Marshall nodded.

"Jim Wade," he said quietly. He hitched up his gun belt, shifted the twin holsters a bit forward as Lewis watched. "Look, Tom, you hustle into th' house through th' back door. Keep Fran away from th' windows, understand? An' that goes fer you, too. If Wade's drunk, he's li'ble t' start blastin' away soon's he gets close enough, an' in his condition th' windows'll be what he'll hit."

"But you watch yourself, y'hear?"

Marshall smiled fleetingly.

"Don't worry about me," he answered. "I c'n take care o' myself awright, an' uv all th' Jim Wades you'll ever see. Go 'head."

Tom trudged away. When he reached the back door and jerked it open, Marshall started up through the alley.

"Marshall!" he heard a thick, gruff voice yell. "Come outta there, you yeller-livered skunk! Come outta there an' get what's comin' to you!"

He was a dozen feet from the entrance to the alley when Jim Wade staggered by. Six or eight townsmen followed at a short distance behind him.

"Marshall!" he heard Jim roar again. "Come outta there, damn you, or I'm comin' in after you!"

He reached the end of the alley. The townsmen had halted behind Jim, and one of them spied Marshall. He nudged the man nearest him, and both paled, wheeled and backed away hastily. The others looked up wonderingly, until they too saw Marshall standing in the alley entrance, his thumbs hooked in his gun belt. There was a sudden and general confusion. In another minute Jim Wade stood alone. His companions halted their flight presently and separated, darting into nearby doorways and peering out.

"Marshall!" Jim roared at the very top of his liquor-thickened voice.

"Wa-al?" Marshall demanded curtly.

Jim stiffened, turned his head slowly, and stared hard at the rigid black-clad man. He blinked once or twice, took a single step forward, stopped, braced himself on widespread legs, and squared his shoulders.

"Marshall," he began again. "I'm gonna kill you!"

'You better go sleep off that drunk before you try it!" Marshall retorted. "You might have a chance then!"

Jim stumbled forward. He tripped mounting the curb, kept his feet somehow, miraculously, and stumbled on. Marshall did not move.

"Marshall!" a voice yelled. "Watch that polecat! He's on'y puttin' on that he's so drunk!"

It was Tom Lewis' voice and Marshall recognized it at once. Then a huge, plunging form leaped over the sidewalk. Marshall sidestepped, struck swiftly, a piledriving, murderous blow that exploded in Jim Wade's face. It was a bone-crushing punch, a paralyzing blow that halted his onrush and left him dazed and tottering. Marshall leaped in again, struck him again... Jim turned away slowly, a battered, bleeding hulk of a man. He stumbled awkwardly, blindly, swayed drunkenly and fell sideways and rolled over. He was near the curb now, and he dragged himself up to his knees, using his big hands and thick arms to prop himself up. He raised his head. His right eye was closed; in fact, the entire right side of his face appeared battered and crushed. There was surprisingly little blood on his face; actually, little more than a trickle on his lips. Slowly he focused his left eye on the tall, lean man who stood so motionlessly now, watching him, and then suddenly Jim's right arm jerked backward. His gun cleared its holster. He snapped it upward in a lightning motion, leveled it, when a Colt thundered deafeningly, drowning out all other sounds. Jim's gun flamed, its report puny by comparison. The bullet ploughed harmlessly into the wooden sidewalk at a point about a yard beyond where Marshall was crouched amid a swirl of gently rising gunsmoke.

Jim's fingers opened and the gun slid out of his hand and dropped on the sidewalk within inches of his left hand. He tottered brokenly and his head came down. He lurched forward, struck on his face, rolled partly over on his back and lay still. The echo of gunfire seemed to linger in the air, spanning the length of the hushed street from one end to the other.

Then there was a sudden rush of booted feet, and two men came dashing up the street. One of them jerked out his gun and snapped a shot that went wild; Marshall fired but once in reply. The second man stopped immediately, turned around in almost the same movement and fled. The man who had fired halted too; his hat had been whisked off his head. He stared at it as it spun over the curb; when it toppled over limply in the gutter, he leaped after it, caught it up and scampered back onto the sidewalk, whirled and plunged headlong into a nearby alley. Now other men emerged from their places of safety. Some of them started toward the out-sprawled Jim Wade on the run. The bank door was suddenly flung open and Tom Lewis, rifle-armed, rushed out.

"Stay where y'are!" he yelled, and leveled his rifle threateningly.

The oncoming men skidded to a hesitant stop. Marshall glanced at them; then he holstered his gun, bent over Jim for a moment, and straightened up again.

"Tom!" he called.

Lewis came to his side at once, looking at him questioningly.

"Put your rifle inside," Marshall instructed him in a low tone. "Then come back here. Want you t' help me get him into th' bank."

"Huh?" Tom's eyes were wide. "What's th' idea?"

"Do's I say," Marshall said curtly. "We'll talk about it afterwards."

"Awright, on'y I think you're plumb loco," Tom flung over his shoulder as he strode away. He returned in another moment without his rifle. "Need a dozen men t' carry that overstuffed buff'lo."

"Never mind th' gab," Marshall snapped. "Take his feet."

Tom scowled darkly; however, he obeyed. He took Jim's feet; then, with Marshall doing the actual carrying, they managed to get Jim into the bank. Fran, wide-eyed and white-faced, met them, and came forward at once to hold the door for them.

"Close it," Marshall panted. "An' lock it."

Fran obeyed without a word of protest.

"Inside," Marshall breathed to Tom. "Put 'im on my bed."

Tom mumbled something under his breath, but his protests were confined to idle mutterings rather than to physical stoppages, and presently Jim Wade was laid out on Marshall's bed.

Mike Gallo had witnessed the entire affair from his own doorway. When he saw Jim Wade drop his gun and pitch forward on his face, he was completely satisfied. He smiled, turned on his heel and went directly to the back room, emerging a minute later with his hat on his head and his coat slung over his arm. The bartender looked up questioningly.

"Keep an eye on things, Charley," Gallo instructed him.

"Sure, Boss."

" 'Case I ain't back by midnight," Gallo continued, "close up."

"Yeah, but what about th' dough in th' till?"

"I got it," Gallo answered.

"What about th' rest o' th' dought I'm gonna take in b'tween now an' closin' time?"

Gallo smiled coldly.

"T'day's payday, ain't it? Take that dough fer your week's pay," he said, and strode out.

A few minutes later he led his horse out from behind the café. He mounted, settled himself in the saddle, gripped the reins and loped away.

CHAPTER TWELVE

GALLO RIDES AGAIN

IT WAS a clear, bright, starlit and moonlit night, with a brisk, fresh coolness in the air. Gallo's mount dashed along spiritedly, his hoof beats echoing over the shale upgrade that led to the Bar-O. Topping the grade, Gallo could see yellowish lights on the lower floor of the ranch-house, evidence that the Wades were still awake. He clattered past the bunkhouse, a low, squat, almost shapeless structure, distorted because it was in darkness, and swung around the corral at a loping pace. He could hear the horses in the corral milling about; now, too, he saw half a dozen figures perched on the top rail of the corral.

"Sure stay up late out here," he muttered to himself. He slackened his horse's pace when they came abreast of the late sitters. "Hi, there! Ed up at th' house?"

"Yep!" a voice answered. "An' who wants t' know?"

"Me!" Mike called over his shoulder as he spurred away. Presently he whirled up to the front porch, reined in, dismounted and had started up the steps when the door opened and a burly, shirtsleeved figure appeared in the doorway.

"Evenin', Ed," Gallo called.

"Huh?" Ed answered. Mike stopped on the top step and pushed his hat back from his eyes. Ed laughed. "Oh, h'llo, Mike! Thought you were Jim at first; then I knew it couldn't be. He was never that p'lite in his hull life. Don't believe I ever heard him say 'good evenin' ' t' anybody! Hey, what are you doin' out this way, huh?"

"Wanted t' see you."

"Uh-huh. I'm just tryin' t' recall when you were out here last. Must be years now, Mike. Probably when th' old man died—right?"

"Yeah, reckon that's right, Ed."

Ed pushed the door open.

"Go 'head, Mike. Into th' kitchen. We c'n talk in there," he said.

They trooped into the house, reached the kitchen. Ed closed the door behind him, nodded toward a chair at the table.

"Sit down."

Mike swung a chair away from the table, seated himself and looked up. Ed sat down on the opposite side of the table.

"Have a drink?" he asked. "It oughta be good. I got it from you, y'know."

"Not right now."

Ed sat back in his chair.

"Whatever you say," he said. "How's tricks in Rainbow?"

"Could be better, heaps better."

"That Marshall feller still around?"

Gallo nodded mutely.

"Sure wish somebody would do me a big favor an' put a bullet in him where it'd do him th' most harm an' me th' most good," Ed said with a grin. He eyed Mike sharply. "What th' hell's th' matter with you, huh?"

"Ed," Mike said heavily, "I gotta tell you somethin' an' I wish t' God I didn't hafta."

"What is it?"

"Wa-al, it's funny you wishin' just a minute ago that somebody'd take a shot at Marshall, because somebody did."

Wade laughed lightly.

"On th' level? Who was it?" he demanded interestedly.

Gallo drew a deep breath.

"Jim," he said quietly, and waited.

"Jim?" Ed repeated. "Th' hell he did! Why, that danged, locoed fool! He couldn't hit th' broad side uv a barn with a gun 'less he stood right on top uv it!"

"Wa-al, he tried t' do a job on Marshall, so you gotta give 'im credit fer that."

"Yeah, I suppose so. But doggone it, Mike, I'd expect you t' stick up fer Jim—fer anybody fer that matter. You're th' doggonedest feller! You allus see good in everybody, don't you?"

Gallo averted his eyes.

"Was that what you come all th' way out here t' tell me?" Ed asked. "Oh, I get it. You wanted t' tell me about it yourself so's I'd be calmed down by th' time Jim got home. Doggone you, Mike! You're awright an' I wish t' hell there were more like you!"

"There's more t' th' story, Ed."

"Then spill it, man! I c'n take it."

"I better begin from th' b'ginnmg," Gallo said, and Ed nodded. "Jim come into th' Star 'round evenin'. He had a couple o' drinks an' pretty soon his tongue got loosened up an' he nearly floored me by spoutin' out loud that he was out t' kill Marshall. 'Course I tried t' talk 'im outta th' idea, but you know how liquor c'n give a feller funny ideas."

"Go on, Mike."

"Wa-al, there wasn't any talkin' him outta what he'd cooked up," Gallo continued, "so I got an idea myself. I figgered that if he got good an' cockeyed, he'd ferget th' hull thing. I give th' bartender th' eye, an' when Jim finished one bottle, another one was set up for 'im. I even went upstairs an' fixed up a place fer him t' sleep. I figgered he'd sleep off 'is drunk an' then by mornin' when he woke up, th' idea'd be gone."

Ed nodded approvingly.

"Uh-huh. What happened?"

"Th' place kinda busied up an' I turned away from Jim fer a couple o' minutes. Th' next thing I knowed he was out th' door an' headin' up th' street tow'rd th' bank."

Ed was silent, waiting for Mike to go on.

"Wa-al, I went after Jim but he had too much uv a lead on me. Besides, he musta run right smack into Marshall in th' street, judging by how fast things happened. Jim hauled off on Marshall, but like I told you, Ed, he was pretty drunk an' Marshall walloped him plenty."

"Th' dirty skunk," Ed gritted. "Wallopin' a drunk who couldn't fight back!"

"Jim went down on 'is knees but he wasn't through. Nope, he had plenty o' guts, too much fer 'is own good. He went fer 'is gun, but Marshall beat 'em to th' draw an' blasted 'im."

Ed was on his feet now. His eyes were blazing.

"By God!" he stormed. "I'll kill 'im fer that!"

Mike arose too. He pushed the chair closer to the table.

"Ed, Jim's dead," he said quietly.

"I figgered he was," Ed said heavily, "judgin' by th' way you led up to it."

Gallo breathed a sigh of relief.

"But I ain't blamin' you fer any uv it, Mike," Ed added. "You done all you could an' mebbe more an' I won't ferget it, believe me."

"We're friends, Ed, an' friends are supposed t' do whatever they can an' whenever they get th' chance to."

"Yeah, I suppose so."

"Ed, now that you know 'bout Jim, what are you gonna do?"

"Dunno yet, Mike. 'Course I know there's actu'lly on'y one thing to do an' that is fer me t' kill Marshall."

"But—?"

"He's a smart hombre. I can't afford t' leave anythin' t' chance. I gotta figger out all th' angles an' everything I'm gonna do so no matter what he does I'll be prepared fer it."

"Uh-huh. Ord'narily I'd say that was th' on'y way t' tackle 'im."

"An' now?"

"No good."

"Awright. What's your idea?"

"Wa-al, this is th' way I'd figger it. Here Marshall's just killed your brother. He's smart like you say he is, so he knows you're gonna do somethin' about squarin' accounts with 'im an' pronto. He's worried an' jumpy. He's prob'bly stayin' up all night t' night, an' every sound he hears, he figgers it's you."

"Go on."

"He'll probably have a couple o' shots o' whiskey t' steady 'imself, but by th' time mornin' comes rollin' around, he'll have finished a hull bottle full. He'll be so blamed bleary-eyed, he won't be fit fer anything. It's common sense, Ed, leastways it is t' me, that worry, no sleep an' a good-sized swig o' liquor thrown in every now an' then c'n do more t' ruin a feller, an' quicker, too, than anything else you ever heard tell uv."

"Suppose that's right, Mike. You figger that mornin' would be—"

"Nope," Gallo said, interrupting him. "Sunup."

"Awright, sunup."

"Yep," Mike said with finality. "He'll be at 'is worst at sunup, sleepier'n all hell. That's when you wanna tackle 'im. What's more, Ed, this is th' kind uva job that wants on'y one feller t' do it. So th' thing fer you t' do is do it an' th' sooner th' better. Puttin' it off—"

"I don't aim t' put it off."

"Good fer you. In that case—"

"I'm plannin' t' hit Rainbow t'morrow mornin' at sunup," Ed concluded. "An' I'll be alone, too."

Gallo nodded, turned, trudged to the door and opened it. Wade followed him out, and they halted again when they reached the front door.

"G'night, Ed."

"G'night, Mike, an' thanks fer everything."

"Ferget it," Gallo answered, and went out.

He mounted slowly, heavily, with unusual and evidently purposeful deliberation, wheeled his horse away from the house, jogged toward the corral, circled it. There was no noisy milling about. The horses had quieted down; he could see them now, shadowy and indistinct, huddling together at the far end of the enclosure. He noticed at a glance that the late sitters had gone. He twisted around in the saddle and looked toward the bunkhouse. A dimmed light gleamed in its single window and cast a thin ray of yellowish light over the ground below it. The corral fell away behind him, and he shot a quick look over his shoulder.

A slim, cloaked figure appeared at that moment in a breathless, diagonal dash from the direction of the rear of the house.

"There she is," he muttered.

In another moment the girl spotted him and she swerved toward him. He drew rein and waited, eased himself in the saddle until she came panting up to him.

"Mike!" she said breathlessly.

"H'llo, Eadie," he answered. "I had a hunch you'd be wantin' t' see me after I left th' house, so I kinda moseyed along slow's I could t' give you a chance t' get out here ahead o' me."

"You mean you knew I was—"

"Oh, sure!" he said laughingly. "I saw you standin' behind th' curtain between th' kitchen an' th' parlor. Fact o' th' matter is, Eadie, I spotted you standin' there th' minute I come in."

"Oh!"

"When I sat down," he continued, "I took th' chair facin' in your direction 'stead o' leavin' that one fer Ed. He hadda walk 'round th' table t' get to th' other chair, an' when he sat down he had 'is back t' you."

"I couldn't tell that, Mike. I didn't dare peek out."

"Uh-huh. What'd you wanna see me about, Eadie?"

"Does Ed know that I—"

"That it was you who rode into Rainbow an' warned Marshall that Jim was comin' fer 'im? Nope."

"It was sweet of you, Mike, not to tell him that."

"An' if he ever finds it out, I'll tell 'im you came t' tell me about Jim so's I could try t' stop 'im. That'll satisfy 'im."

"Oh, Mike! You're an angel!"

"Oh, sure!" he said, and laughed. "You'd better be gettin' back t' th' house, Eadie. It's late. An' don't you go worryin' about anything. Y'hear?"

"Yes, Mike, and thanks loads."

"Ferget it. G'night!"

He spurred his horse and sent him dashing away into the night.

It was three o'clock in the morning. Rainbow was hushed and gloomily dark. There was a sudden clatter of hoofs; then a lone horseman appeared and came loping down the street. He peered intently, sharply, in the night light at every store sign he passed, then halted his mount abruptly, wheeled and came jogging back, and pulled up in front of the bank. He dismounted stiffly; for a moment he looked up and down the street. When he seemed satisfied that he had aroused no one, he marched briskly across the sidewalk. He stopped at the door, reached for the knob, checked himself, considered briefly, then rapped on the door lightly. There was a minute-long wait; finally the door was opened.

"Smith!" Marshall greeted him in a low, guarded tone.

"Hi, feller!"

"Come alone?"

"Uh-huh. That's th' way you wanted it, wasn't it?"

"That's right. Figgered nobody'd think anything if they spotted you. A hull troop o' riders'd be sure t' 'rouse th' town, an' then everybody'd know what was cookin'," Marshall answered. "Hey! Where's Tom Lewis?"

"Who? Oh, y'mean th' ol' feller you sent t' get me? Heck, he was so plumb tuckered out after that long ride, I made 'im stay put fer th' rest o' th' night. He'll probably be showin' up later on or soon's he feels up t' ridin' back. Say, don't a feller get invited inside?"

"Sure, Smith," Marshall said quickly. "Figered we'd do our talkin' out here first, then we'd go in an' see what we c'n do with Wade."

"Oh, I get it. You think th' polecat'll open up?"

"Yeah, I think he will."

"Awright. What's th' set-up?"

"Wa-al, I got an idea th' minute he knows he's up against Ranger law, he's gonna bust wide open. While he's stewin' in his own juice, you an' me c'n kinda jaw a lot about hangin' 'im. You c'n be stiff an' hard while I try t' proposition you on a deal fer him if he talks. How's that sound t' you?"

"Awright, I guess, Marsh. Anyway, it's worth a try."

"Then let's go inside."

Smith Jenkins stepped into the bank. He closed the door behind him noiselessly; then he followed Marshall through darkened rooms. He blinked and slackened his pace when they came into the light.

"Here's your man, Smith," he heard Marshall say.

They were in a small room. There were two cots in it, with a single chair between them. In the middle of the room was a table with a lighted lamp on top of it. On one cot lay a bulky, blanket-covered man with a scowl on his face and a bloodstained bandage wound around his head. He glared at the newcomer, who eyed him coldly, disdainfully.

"This is Jim Wade," Marshall said presently. "I dunno fer sure yet whether he's lucky my bullet on'y clipped 'is head an' left 'im alive so's th' law c'n hang 'im, or not."

Jenkins moved closer to the big man and looked down at him, and Jim's eyes widened suddenly. He had spied the gold badge on Smith's shirt-front and now he was staring at it.

"So you're Jim Wade, eh?" Smith mused.

"You a Ranger?"

Jenkins nodded grimly.

"Yep," he said curtly. "Lieutenant."

Wade's face seemed strangely white. In the yellow lamplight it was pasty.

"Awright, Marshall!" Smith said. "Let's get him up on 'is feet an' be on our way!"

"Where—where you takin' me?" Jim asked in a hollow, unfamiliar voice.

"To a hangin'!" Smith snapped in reply. "Yours!"

Jim gulped and swallowed hard.

"Wait a minute, Jenkins!" Marshall said quickly. "Can't we make some kind o' deal fer him?"

"Th' law don't make deals fer killers an' bank robbers!"

"Yeah," Marshall said. "I know that. But, doggone it, man, this is diff'rent."

"Not th' way I see it," Smith retorted. "This feller an' 'is brother've been raisin' all kinds o' hell 'round these parts fer a long time. Now we've caught up with 'im an' he'll hafta pay fer th' things he's done."

"Wa-al," Marshall began slowly, "s'ppose he wants t' do somethin' decent?"

Jenkins' lip curled scornfully.

"He wouldn't know how!" he said coldly.

"You don't understand," Marshall said quickly. "Suppose he wants t' face th' law with a clear conscience? Suppose he wants t' tell everything he knows?"

"Let 'im!"

"If he does, what'll you do fer him in return?"

"Look, Marshall," Smith said with finality. "I dunno what th' hell you're drivin' at. What's more, I ain't in-t'rested. But I'm allus willin' t' give everybody a fair shake. If this feller's got somethin' t' say an' if he starts talkin' th' minute I'm finished an' comes through with everything he knows—"

"Yeah? What then?"

"I won't make any promises. All I'll say is that I'll talk up fer 'im where it'll do 'im good."

"There y'are, Wade," Marshall said, turning to him. "It's up t' you now. You're gettin' a helluva better break th'n you deserve. So now you better start talkin' or—"

"He'll hang!" Smith concluded and turned away.

Jim Wade gulped again, loudly and painfully, and swallowed hard.

"Wa-al?" Marshall demanded impatiently.

"Awright," Jim wheezed. "What d'you want me t' tell you?"

CHAPTER THIRTEEN
THE GOOD SAMARITAN

The first gray light of dawn pierced the dull sky, and the last lingering night shadows vanished. The air was chilly and a swift, noisy breeze droned through Rainbow, swirling dust in its wake. Mike Gallo appeared in the doorway of his café. He looked eastward anxiously, listened intently and finally shrugged.

"Hope t' hell he don't get cold feet," he muttered to himself. "That'd sure be one helluva note, just when I got things fixed."

He heard a hoof beat and dashed into the street; a horseman came whirling into view. Gallo's heart pounded wildly. It was Ed Wade, and Mike's anxiety vanished.

"He's come awright!" he told himself delightedly. "He's come!"

Wade slackened his horse's pace for a moment, spied Gallo and he rode forward again, guiding his mount to where Mike was awaiting him. He clattered up and reined in.

"Got here like I said I would," he said simply.

"Uh-huh," Gallo answered. "Better climb down now, Ed."

"Huh? Why?"

"I figger it might be better if I was t' go take a look first," Gallo explained. "Wanna see if Marshall's around an' what he's doin'. I don't aim t' let you get shot up like Jim was. Anyway, soon's I know it's awright, I'll come back fer you an' you c'n go 'head an' do what you gotta. Get th' idea?"

"Yeah, sure, Mike," Ed replied. He swung himself out of the saddle. "Want me t' wait here?"

"No," Gallo said. "Take your horse 'round th' back o' my place; then you c'n wait fer me just inside th' alley-way. Might be a good idea fer you t' stay outta sight complete till it's time fer you t' come out in th' open."

Ed nodded in agreement.

"Whatever you say, Mike. You're runnin' this thing an' you sure seem t' know what's t' be done. Awright, I'll go 'round t' th' back an' meet you in th' alley."

They turned as one. Wade led his horse onto the sidewalk; then he disappeared into the alley that led to the lean-to behind the café. Gallo strode briskly down the street, crossing diagonally to the opposite side, then continuing until he reached the bank. He halted in front of it, turned and looked up the street for a brief moment, then wheeled and marched into the alley that flanked the bank. He quickened his pace, whirled round the building to the back door and knocked on it impatiently. There was a brief wait. Presently he heard a heavy step inside; a key grated in the lock and a bolt was drawn back; then the door was opened. Marshall, his hand on his gun butt, eyed him questioningly.

"Oh, it's you, eh?"

"Yep, an' I gotta see you 'bout somethin'."

Marshall frowned with annoyance.

"Kinda early t' be out visitin', ain't it?" he asked.

"I didn't come here t' pay you a visit," he said a bit sharply. "I'm here because I figgered you oughta know that Ed Wade's in town."

Marshall's eyebrows arched.

"Ed Wade, eh?" he repeated thoughtfully, and frowned again.

"I don't suppose I hafta tell you what he's here for," Gallo added.

"Nope," Marshall said grimly. "That's one thing I c'n figger out fer myself."

"That's what I thought."

There was a brief silence.

"Where's he at?"

"Down at my place. I slipped away first chance I got so's I could hustle up here an' tell you 'bout it."

"Uh-huh. What's he doin', drinkin'?"

"Nope," Gallo answered. "He's cold sober."

"Wa-al, thanks fer th' tip, Gallo."

The café owner grinned fleetingly.

"Ferget it. I just don't aim t' have anything that I c'n prevent happen to you. That's all."

"I don't either," Marshall replied.

"Look, Marshall, Ed'll be heaps diff'rent than Jim was. I mean you'll hafta handle Ed diff'rent."

"I don't get that."

"Wa-al, what I was tryin' t' say was that Ed's smart. Just give him th' slightest break an' you'll be deader'n all hell. He's damned good with a six-gun—fast, an' what's worse, tricky."

"Y'mean I'll hafta watch 'im every minute o' th' time I'm near 'im. That th' idea?"

"On'y part uv it. My idea is t' cut loose with them Colts o' yourn th' minute he comes close enough. He's out t' kill you an' I don't see why'n hell you should give 'im even th' slightest chance t' draw. Get 'im while th' gettin' is good an' you'll be done with th' Wades fer good."

"I see."

"Believe me, Marshall, I know what I'm talkin' about. Th' Wades were never ones t' give th' other feller a break. That's why Boothill's so danged overcrowded now with other fellers. You do like they done an' they'll be plantin' you there, too."

"You figger Ed's gonna come after me?" Marshall asked.

"I know he is," Gallo answered quickly. "I heard 'im say so."

"Uh-huh."

"But that's a break fer you right off," Gallo went on. "He's gotta come t' you an' you c'n start blastin' away at him th' minute he reaches here. Hell, you c'n be behind somethin' an' he'll hafta spot you before ne c'n start shootin' back at you"

Marshall listened attentively. He looked at Gallo, quietly studying the big man. He made no comment, waited instead for Gallo to continue.

"So there y'are," Mike concluded. "You know what you're facin'. You know what you gotta do an' th' best way t' do it. When it's done, mebbe then we c'n have some peace 'round these parts."

"Awright, Gallo, an' thanks again fer tippin' me off."

"Never mind th' thanks. Just remember that it's your life or Ed Wade's an' act accordin'."

"I intend to."

Gallo nodded, turned abruptly and strode around the building. Marshall heard the big man's quick step in the alley; in another minute it faded away completely.

Ed wade, a big, tight-lipped man with quick, anxious eyes and a nervous, tense impatience about him, was waiting in the alley-way when Gallo came striding in from the street. Ed looked up quickly and came forward at once.

"Awright?" he asked.

"Yep!" Gallo panted in answer.

Wade nodded. He hitched up his belt mechanically, jerked out his gun as Mike watched, palmed it expertly and fanned it skillfully, then slipped the weapon back into its holster. Gallo grinned.

"That's awright, Ed!" he said admiringly. "You're even faster with a gun than I figgered. I got an idea this is gonna be easier'n you're willin' t' believe."

Wade did not answer. He shifted his holster a bit until the butt of his gun was directly below his fingers.

"You see 'im?" he asked.

Mike nodded mutely.

"How'd he look? Like you figgered he would?"

"Huh? Oh, sure! He looked like somethin' that rode into town on th' buckin' tail uva cyclone!"

Ed grinned fleetingly.

"Think he had a tough night, eh?"

"An' how!" Gallo answered. "Tryin' t' stay awake an' hittin' th' bottle at th' same time—wa-al, you c'n imagine what he looks like. You'll see fer yourself soon enough. You oughta get goin', Ed."

"Yeah, in a minute. Which way d'you think I oughta bust in on 'im, Mike, from th' back?"

"Heck, no!" Gallo said quickly. "Go in through th' front door. He won't be expectin' you t' bust in that way an' you'll take 'im by s'prise."

"Uh-huh."

"An' start shootin' th' minute you get inside an' see anythin' that looks like him. Don't ferget that!"

Ed grinned again, lightly.

"You ever hear o' me givin' a skunk a break?" he asked.

Gallo laughed softly and patted him on the back.

"Nope," he replied. "Never. Now go ahead, Ed. Go get 'im an' when you come back we'll celebrate."

Wade hitched up his belt again and squared his shoulders.

"Be seein' you," he said, and trudged out to the street. Ed Wade was twenty feet from the bank when the door opened and Marshall emerged. Ed halted abruptly. His hand dropped instantly to his gun butt. Marshall, his hands dangling at his sides, stepped into the gutter, turned and looked up. Ed seemed uncertain, even hesitant; then his right arm jerked suddenly. His gun flashed in his hand; the muzzle cleared the thick leather lip of his holster and snapped upward. He fired and the rolling echo of gunfire filled the air, ranged the length of the street; there was an answering roar and the echo swelled mightily for an instant, burst and started to fade, leaving in its wake a curious, muffled rumbling that sounded like distant summer thunder. Then in another moment the rumbling too had gone.

Ed staggered. He braced himself with an effort, even squared his shoulders. His gun came down now and slid out of his hand, dropped limply into the gutter. He turned clumsily, managing to keep his feet when it appeared that he would fall, and started up the street at a stumbling, faltering, foot-dragging pace. He swerved blindly toward the curb, mounted it and stopped. Again he braced himself, and went on. He reached an alley, turned into it, disappeared. A minute later he reappeared, stumbling out, his hands clutching at his chest. He sagged and crumpled and fell on his hands and knees, stiffened and pitched forward on his face.

There was a sudden banging of doors and presently men with tousled heads and sleep-reddened eyes peered out. Marshall, his gun holstered, came striding up the street. Men eyed him; others stared at the limp, out-sprawled figure on the sidewalk. Half a dozen men stepped out into the street. When Marshall passed them, they fell in behind him silently, following at his heels. He stopped beside Ed and looked down at him; another man dropped to one knee, bent over Wade and turned him over on his broad back. There were two wide, soggy bloodstains on Ed's shirt-front. The man nodded, looked up, caught Marshall's eye and nodded again.

"Got 'im plumb center, Mister," he said, and climbed to his feet. "Your first shot on'y winged 'im, probably busted 'is shoulder. But th' second one done th' trick awright, drilled 'im clean through th' heart."

There was a frown on Marshall's face. His eyes ranged over the faces of the men around him. He turned, stopped when he heard the pounding of running feet, and looked back over his shoulder. He saw Mike Gallo coming down the street on the run. But he did not wait. He shouldered his way out of the circle of men and strode away. He was within a dozen feet of the bank when the door was flung open and Tom Lewis, his rifle gripped in one hand, and his pants held up by the other, dashed out.

"Hey!" Tom yelled, and skidded to a stop. He looked at Marshall, then past him. After a moment he looked up at Marshall again and grinned. "Reckon that's that, eh?"

"Yep," Marshall answered. "Ed Wade's dead."

"Sure looks like it from here," Tom said, and he laughed softly. "Y'know, Marshall, I've hated that polecat ever since I c'n remember. I've allus hoped I'd be on hand when he got what was comin' to 'im. I wanted t' be right there to see him stop a bullet in 'is gizzard, wanted t' see 'im suffer like he made others suffer. But I don't feel bad about it now, I mean about not bein' on hand t' see how it happened to 'im. Long's I know he's dead an' that it was you who done it, I—"

"I didn't do it, Tom," Marshall said, interrupting him. "I hate t' disappoint you, but somebody else did th' job."

The old man stared hard at him.

"Huh? What was that?" he demanded. "Gimme that again."

"I said I didn't kill him," Marshall said patiently. "Somebody else did."

"I—I don't get it."

"That makes two uv us that don't get it," Marshall said grimly. "I fired at 'im, awright, an' I know I hit 'im. But I on'y fired once an' I hit 'im in th' shoulder. I wanted t' get him alive, not dead, but somebody else had diff'rent ideas an' beat me to 'im."

"An' there's another hole in 'im beside yourn?" Tom asked.

"Marshall nodded.

"Right over th' heart," he replied.

"Wonder who else had th' guts t' go after 'im?"

"While you're figgerin' that one out," Marshall said dryly, "try your hand at th' next question. There were on'y two shots fired—leastways that's all I heard—Wade's an' mine. I not on'y didn't hear th' shot that killed Wade, but I'm doggoned if I c'n even figger out where it come from. Mebbe you c'n figger it out for me, Tom. I can't. I'm stumped an' I mean it."

"Wait a minute!" Tom commanded. "Lemme get th' picture set in my mind. Did you see anybody?"

"Nope. That is, nobody but Gallo, an' that was when he come t' warn me that Ed was here. But Gallo went back t' his place, an' then th' next time I saw 'im it was after th' killin' an' Gallo was runnin' down t' street t' where Wade was layin'. That lets him out. He couldn'ta done it."

Tom turned away.

"C'mon," he said over his shoulder. "Let's go fix us some breakfast. I'm doggoned hungry."

CHAPTER FOURTEEN
THE SUM TOTAL

OLD TOM LEWIS idled in the doorway between the bank and the living quarters, watching Fran as she swept the bank floor.

"Y'know," he mused, "it's doggoned funny 'bout Marshall. Y'know that, Fran?"

"Funny?" she repeated without looking up. "What do you mean?"

"Wa-al, I went down th' street with 'im a while ago, an' I'm doggoned if every woman we passed, young an' old alike, didn't turn aroun' an' give 'im th' eye."

"Really?"

"Yep. I suppose there is somethin' about 'im that makes women folks do like they do when he comes along. There must be. I ain't never noticed 'specially, but I suppose t' them he's kind o' nice-lookin'."

"I think he's a very good-looking man."

"Uh-huh. Then, too, he's big an' carries 'imself—"

"Like an athlete, Tom, and all women want their men to look like that."

"Yeah, I suppose that's right, Fran. But I'll say this much fer him—he didn't give any o' th'm a tumble."

She did not answer. He watched her out of the corner of his eye, saw a fleeting smile tug at the corners of her mouth.

"Bet there'll be a heap o' busted hearts 'round these parts when he pulls up stakes an' moves on," he mused again.

Fran looked up quickly. Tom saw at once that the smile had gone.

"Has he—has he said anything about that to you?" she asked.

He shook his head.

"Nope. I'm just readin' th' signs, that's all."

"Oh!" she said quickly, relief in her voice.

"He ain't th' kind t' stay put around a hole like Rainbow," he went on doggedly. "He's too big fer us. He oughta be runnin' one o' them big ranches like they got in Texas an' other places. Just you watch an' see if I ain't right about him pullin' outta here one o' these days. There's nuthin' fer 'im here an' there never will be."

She smiled quietly, confidently.

"And yet, Tom," she said, "he might find something in Rainbow to hold his interest. Something no one else even suspects. He might, you know"

Tom shook his head.

"I wouldn't count on that a-tall," he said with finality. "That feller's meant fer bigger things than Rainbow c'n ever offer 'im, an' 'less I miss my guess complete, Fran, he's gonna get th'm."

"Perhaps. Tom, do you remember what Dad used to say about the grass being greener in the other fellow's yard?" she asked.

Tom grinned sheepishly.

"He used t' say so many things I ain't sure that I remember that partic'lar one," he replied. "What was it?"

" 'Clover,' Dad said, 'was where you found it.' "

"Huh?"

"That means that a man doesn't have to leave his own back yard to find the things he wants most. I believe that, Tom. Usually those very things are right there, simply waiting for him to realize that they are there. Sometimes, of course, someone else has to point them out to him. However, eventually he discovers their existence, one way or another."

Tom suddenly straightened up.

"We're gettin' comp'ny," he said.

The street door opened as Fran turned. In the open doorway stood a pretty, smiling young woman. Tom stared at her, gulped and swallowed. Hastily he backed out of sight, wheeled and fled.

"Hello."

Fran eyed her, and the newcomer in turn eyed Fran. She seemed to focus her eyes first on the broom in Fran's hand, then on the torn towel she had wound around her hair to protect it from the dust. Fran followed the young woman's eyes and frowned.

"Yes?"

"I'm looking for someone—a man."

"Indeed!" Fran said sarcastically.

"His name is Marshall. I understand he lives here."

"That's right—he does live here."

"Well, is he here now, or can you tell me where I might find him?"

"Is he expecting you?" Fran countered.

"Oh, no!" the other woman said quickly. "I thought I'd just run in on him and surprise him."

"In that case," Fran said frigidly, "I'm afraid I can't help you very much. However, if you care to leave your name or a message—"

"No, I don't think I ought to do that. Actually, he might not approve of my coming here at all. Of course, if he were here now—"

Fran frowned again. Suddenly she recalled what Tom had told her earlier about the women on the street who had turned and looked so brazenly at Marshall. Her eyes glinted; she was certain that this young woman was one of them. "Perhaps then," she said coldly, "it's just as well that he isn't here now."

"Oh, really?"

"Yes," Fran went on. "Since you won't leave any word for him, and since you seem to doubt that he would be pleased to see you here, perhaps it would be best if you didn't come back. I'm sure if he were anxious to see you he would know how to get in touch with you."

"I see," the young woman said slowly. "Has anyone ever told you that you're a very impertinent person? Actually, you act as if you owned him and made up his mind for him. You sound like a wife, or however a nasty-tongued wife is supposed to sound."

Fran's eyes blazed.

"I'm not at all interested in your opinion of me," she said furiously. "But I do think you'd have more pride than to run after a man and try to force yourself upon him. There are several cafés and saloons down the street. You might try them. I'm sure you'd have greater success there. The men who frequent those places are doubtless better suited to you and your style. You'll excuse me, please. I'm very busy."

Fran turned away and began to ply her broom vigorously. She heard the door close and she smiled to herself. There was a hesitant, cautious step in the connecting doorway and she looked up. It was Tom Lewis.

"She—she gone?" he asked in a guarded tone.

"Yes!" Fran said, and she laughed. "Why, that brazen thing! The nerve of her, coming here after Marshall! But she won't come here again, believe me!"

"Y'mean you—" His voice trailed away weakly.

She laughed again, lightly.

"As you would say, Tom, I 'told her off'!"

He sank back against the door jamb.

"She was just one of those women you told me about, the ones who ogled Marshall on the street."

He struggled, forcing himself upright again with an effort.

"Fran...."

"Yes?"

"It wasn't your fault," he sputtered. "It was all mine an' I oughta get kicked clear outta town. Y'see, I was tryin' t' lead up t' her, on'y I just couldn't seem t' get to it without hurtin' you."

"What do you mean?"

"Fran, she wasn't one o' them women a-tall."

Her eyes widened, and she caught her breath as she waited for him to continue.

"She wasn't?"

" 'Course not! She's Marshall's wife! Doggone an' damnation!"

The Star Café was deserted when Marshall halted in front of it and peered in. He spied Mike Gallo standing behind the bar and sauntered inside. Gallo looked up.

"H'llo, Marshall," he said, and added a smile. "You're just th' feller I've been waitin' t' see. Kinda hoped you'd come by so's we could have a drink t'gether t' sort o' celebrate. This is a big day fer Rainbow an' an even bigger one fer me, now that Ed Wade's gone, an' that sure calls fer some kind o' celebration. An' bein' that you're th' feller responsible fer it all, th' Star's standing' treat."

He bent down, and when he straightened up again, he had a bottle of whiskey in his hand. He uncorked it and placed it on the bar, followed it with two glasses.

"There y'are," he said, and smiled again. "It's my own stuff so you don't hafta be afraid uv it. Go on, man—pour your own."

Marshall did not move. He stood erect, his thumbs hooked in his gun belt. Gallo eyed him questioningly.

"S'matter?" he asked.

"Nuthin' much," Marshall replied. "But suppose we cut out th' horsin' around about celebrations an' talk turkey. You know well's I do, Gallo, that I didn't kill Ed Wade."

The café owner's eyes did not waver.

"Awright," he said quietly. "I killed 'im."

"That's what I figgered," Marshall said calmly.

Gallo was grim-faced now, and tight-lipped.

"Sure I killed Ed," he repeated. "An' I'm glad I did. I've hated his guts fer years, on'y there wasn't anything I could do about it 'cept wait an' hope fer a chance t' come along so's I could pay 'im off. Wa-al, I got th' chance an' he got what was comin' to 'im. Reckon that's about all there was to it."

Marshall nodded understandingly.

"Uh-huh," he said. "Y'know, Gallo, at first I was plumb stopped. I coulda sworn there were on'y two shots fired, Ed's an' mine. An' when I got a quick look at 'im layin' out there in th' street an' found there were two wounds in 'im 'stead o' one, I couldn't figger it out. I didn't hear any third shot, an' what was worse, there wasn't anybody aroun' fer me t' blame it on."

Gallo smiled fleetingly.

"Th' blood covered up both wounds an' I didn't think o' lookin' t' see if both o' th'm were bullet wounds. Reckon I just took it fer granted that they were an' let it go at that. It was on'y afterwards when I got t' thinkin' about it again that I decided I'd better have another look at 'im. I'd heard they'd toted Ed down t' th' sheriff's office, an' I went down there an' took a second look at 'im. Then I knew I wasn't wrong. There wasn't any third shot. What killed Ed was a knife jab straight into 'is heart."

Gallo's smile had vanished.

"Go on," he said briefly.

"Th' funny thing about it," Marshall continued, "was th' fact that even though I knew what'd killed 'im, I was still just as far away from figgerin' out who it was that killed 'im as I was in th' beginnin'. Ordinarily, y'know, one thing allus leads to another. But in this case it was diff'rent. There wasn't any trail t' follow."

There was no comment from Gallo, no movement of any kind. He was motionless, his eyes focused on Marshall's face.

"I went over th' hull thing in my mind, from th' beginnin' right down t' th' end, an' th' on'y one I allus came back to was you, Gallo. Not that that helped any. What made me wind up with you was th' fact that you'd come t' warn me about Ed an' how you'd suggested that I start blastin' away at 'im th' minute I saw 'im an' so on. Somehow that made some kind o' tie-up b'tween you an' th' killin', on'y I couldn't figger out what it was. What threw me off alt'gether was seein' you come runnin' down th' street. I couldn't understand how you could've killed Ed, hustled back t' your place an' then come gallopin' back down th' street again all inside uv a couple o' minutes or mebbe less."

Gallo laughed softly.

"But somehow, everything allus seems t' come out in th' wash. It came t' me all uva sudden. You must've slipped outta here right after Ed did; on'y you worked your way down toward th' bank through th' back yards. You hopped into that alley an', as luck would have it, Ed came stumblin' past there. You must've called to 'im; otherwise I don't think he'da gone in there. Anyway, he went in an' you knifed 'im."

Marshall paused and moistened his lips; then he went on again.

"Mebbe he fell down, mebbe he didn't—not that it makes any diff'rence either way 'cept that it took 'im more'n a full minute t' come outta there. That gave you time t' run like hell through th' yards; then you came out t' th' street again through still another alley further up th' street. You didn't go back t' your place, Gallo. You on'y made it look that way an' I was dumb enough t' fall fer it."

"Awright," Gallo said. "That's close enough t' th' way it happened. So what? I killed th' polecat an' I've admitted it, ain't I? I had damned good reason fer doin' it an' no jury in th' world'd convict me fer it."

"You had a better reason fer killin' Ed," Marshall said quietly, "same's you had fer wantin' Jim Wade killed off."

"Yeah? What was that?"

"Y'see, Gallo," Marshall continued, "you hadda miss up somewheres. Jim ain't dead. He's in jail."

"No!"

"I say he is. Th' Rangers've got 'im. An' he talked, Gallo, heaps. He spilled th' beans 'bout th' bank robbery an' told us—"

"Us?" Gallo echoed. "Y'mean you too? Then you're a Ranger an' not just on th' loose, lookin' fer a job or somethin'?"

"That's right," Marshall answered. "Jim told us that th' bank money was buried down below here under th' floor an' that you were keepin' it for th'm. You wanted both Jim an' Ed outta th' way so's you could have th' money fer yourself. Reckon that's th' hull story, Gallo, an' you're gonna swing fer it, leastways fer th' murder o' Ed Wade. You'd better come out from behind there. You an' me are goin' fer a ride."

Gallo smiled; his white, even teeth flashed in his swarthy face. He brushed a speck of dust from the lapel of his coat, whirled suddenly, a knife gleamed in his hand. Then he threw it. A Colt thundered deafeningly. Gallo staggered, fell against the shelf behind the bar and a dozen bottles crashed to the floor. He stumbled away, reached the end of the bar, braced himself on it and raised his head. He stiffened suddenly, turned halfway and crashed headlong to the floor. Marshall watched him for a moment; then he turned his head and looked at the wooden post behind him. A long knive quivered in the post barely an inch above his head.

The three horses halted when they reached the top of the hill and their riders twisted around and looked down into Rainbow for the last time.

"S'matter, Marsh?" Smith Jenkins asked with a grin. "Wanna go back an' take that sheriff's job there?"

"No, thanks," Marshall answered quickly. "I've had all I want o' Rainbow. Th' Wades are where they won't do any more harm, Mike Gallo's planted right 'longside o' Ed, an' Fran's got th' bank's money back again."

"Yeah, you sure did all th' gov'nor wanted you t' do an' then some," Jenkins commented. "Still he's gonna be sore when I tell 'im you're done an' finished with th' Rangers."

"But he agreed that this was to be Ned's last Ranger mission," Carol said quickly. "He asked us to postpone our trip to California just long enough for Ned to clean up Rainbow, and now that that's done, we're California bound, the governor notwithstanding."

"Say, Marsh," Smith said. "Them two girls standin' in front o' th' bank watched us all th' way up here. Know th'm?"

"Yeah, sure," Marshall answered. "Th' taller one's Fran Grant an' th' other one's Eadie Wade. They'll probably be good friends again now that Fran's got her money back an' Eadie's got not on'y th' dough ol' man Wade left 'er but Jim's an' Ed's, too. Carol, I'm sure sorry you didn't meet Fran an' Eadie, 'specially Fran. You an' she would've hit it off swell t'gether."

Carol and Smith Jenkins looked at each other quickly and exchanged winks.

"Yeah," Jenkins drawled, "I'll bet they would've, too."

They turned in their saddles as one and rode westward.

THE END

www.ingramcontent.com/pod-product-compliance
Lightning Source LLC
LaVergne TN
LVHW051008080826
845145LV00009B/2508

* 9 7 8 1 9 5 4 8 4 0 6 7 6 *